VOLATILE
MEMORY

VOLATILE MEMORY

SETH HADDON

TOR PUBLISHING GROUP

NEW YORK

VOLATILE MEMORY

Endpaper and interior art by Shutterstock.com

A Tordotcom Book
Published by Tom Doherty Associates / Tor Publishing Group
120 Broadway
New York, NY 10271

www.torpublishinggroup.com

Tor® is a registered trademark of Macmillan Publishing Group, LLC.

EU Representative: Macmillan Publishers Ireland Ltd, 1st Floor, The Liffey Trust Centre, 117–126 Sheriff Street Upper, Dublin 1, DO1 YC43

The Library of Congress Cataloging-in-Publication Data is available upon request.

ISBN 978-1-250-36468-5 (hardcover)
ISBN 978-1-250-42918-6 (Australian)
ISBN 978-1-250-36469-2 (ebook)

Our books may be purchased in bulk for specialty retail/wholesale, literacy, corporate/premium, educational, and subscription box use. Please contact MacmillanSpecialMarkets@macmillan.com.

First Edition: 2025

Printed in the United States of America

10   9   8   7   6   5   4   3   2   1

For all the ghosts of temporary storage.

Remember:
everything not saved will be lost.

VOLATILE MEMORY

1

You weren't the only one to receive the signal, but you were the first to respond. Your fingers moved, in the automatic and unconscious way of a lifelong scavenger, and had already plugged in the coordinates to your dingy spacecraft before you realized where the signal was coming from.

You had a MARK I RABBIT, the oldest and crappiest mask on the market, nearly a decade old by the time you'd bought it, and going on another decade since. You had never been able to afford another one. Not on a scavenger's pay.

A good mask overcame the limitations of the human physiology. New RABBITs gave the wearer prey-animal instincts that meant you were always aware, always vaguely tracking threats in the back of your mind. But your mask's processing was sluggish with age and the expanse of decades of technical improvements. Seconds instead of milliseconds. And that meant *you* were slow in understanding the significance of the signal.

It was coming from Pholan's World, an outskirt moon just within the Beta sector of Corporate Federation territory—a nothing satellite, too freezing for a corporate holdout, and too barren for anything else. No ore to mine. No precious stones. No drinkable water. Pholan's World was a dumping ground for scrap and waste. But this signal was bright and strong, like a scream in the void of space. RABBIT's internal threat system flared in a way you had come to understand as panic, a warning that the signal was potent. New. You played the recording to yourself and felt, for the first time in a while, true excitement.

"*I have a* MARK I HAWK," said the voice.

MARK Is usually indicated old tech. But HAWKs didn't exist. So this—this tech, this signal—felt portentous. A new mask. A new future calling out to you.

The message ended with a teasing challenge. "*Do you want it? Come and get it, scavenger.*"

And something about the call, how the woman said "scavenger," felt spiritual. You knew almost innately that the voice called specifically to you.

The revelation sent you whirring at new speed toward the planet, and your heart was a mess of anticipation and fear. If this signal was right—and it was, you knew what you were doing—then you were about to own something priceless.

That was, if you got to it first.

Though you'd responded quickly, your ship was, put simply, a piece of shit. It would take an hour at this speed. You were lucky you were nearby, but there was no telling how many scavengers had heard it, or how close they were to intercepting it. Your class was close knit, outsiders unified through struggle, though you worried this many credits might erode those bonds. After all, you were only a scavenger because you had to be; the dregs of a system that lauded unchecked capitalism. Many of you were free spirits, or refugees, or born so deep into debt that indentured slavery to a corporate power was inevitable. But you, scavenger, were different. Or were marked different. Corporate Federation punished you for the divide in your body and mind; they called you man when you were woman and you had made your body your own, had altered it to recognize yourself, had evolved to a place of comfort, and this made you unemployable in their eyes. Conformity over comfort. Homogeny over evolution. Anyone altered in such a way proved they were unwilling to comply, and anyone like that was difficult to control.

But this mask was a lottery win. Brand-new technological development, a signal you'd never heard before sent out over the feed; and the way RABBIT responded meant it was *good* quality, a mask with enough power to make RABBIT panic.

When you breached the atmosphere of Pholan's World, you learned others had thought the same.

A flier below you broke apart when a shot pierced something vital. A firestorm blared up toward you, roaring, and you had to yank hard on the controls to veer out of the way. The move sent you careening down at an angle; you got an upside-down vista of the broken flier hurtling to the ground with a droning whine. It crashed in the snow and skidded for a few hundred meters before exploding again.

One down, at least.

You were still nearly a kilometer out from the signal, but there was no hope of getting closer: a large carrier craft circled the air above the site. That giant ship was in poor shape itself, smoking and tilting—its main engine was on fire. But the carrier's impressive guns made you realize, if belatedly, exactly what had shot down that other flier, which was at least a few years younger and sturdier than yours. Your flimsy ship had little hope of survival. Just as you thought this, the carrier noticed you and its guns locked on. In a panic, you fired off one shot, but you watched your photon do nothing more than gently graze the carrier's outer hull.

"Fuck," you said, with a sort of resigned embarrassment. Then the carrier returned fire.

Full throttle, you dived down toward the snow. Three shots from the carrier's state-of-the-art gun cannon screamed overhead, and one clipped you—RABBIT was blaring warnings in your ears and you instinctively put your head down as if the shots were aimed for your flesh and not your ship. Your shitty little craft screamed: it was hit. One of the coolant tanks had been pierced and it was now leaking into the snow, aided by this world's heavy gravity. You were going to have to dump it to get off-world, rely purely on the coolant still in the other tank—but this was all a problem for later. Snow whipped up and blinded you, and you went down with more speed than you should have; metal squealed as you landed, your ship battered but not crippled. You unbuckled yourself and stumbled out, suited up, RABBIT on, with nothing more than your blaster.

You were breathing heavy and fast. RABBIT scanned and told you danger was possible from every fucking angle, which was a useless warning, thank you, RABBIT. You had to tell it to focus only on the signal. RABBIT gave you an unhappy warning klaxon, but a beacon materialized in your vision all the same, an ugly green outline in RABBIT's graphical user interface. The signal's location was uphill. No cover. Fuck it—you started running toward where your prize sat.

Everywhere was noise and clamor. The carrier that had been circling above you creaked and whined loudly, and you looked up in time to watch the pilot evacuate. Something went wrong, though, and the body hurtled down to the snow. The ship tilted dramatically and crashed a few kilometers away in a fiery ball.

With that main threat gone, you started sprinting. Your boots shifted in the deep snow. The expanse of white unnerved you: nothing out here could hide you, no rocks, no ruins. You felt naked, even without the firing ship above you. Other scavengers were here. That was threat enough. So you kept running—until you spotted the corpse.

It was slumped forward in the snow. Two smoking holes had bitten into each other and burrowed through its chest. You kicked it over and froze, because the body was wearing a MARK III RATTLESNAKE. A few years ago that had been top-end work. Rapid-snap jaw, poison-coated teeth, all the stuff that made them popular with people starting fights. Only this one had been left as bait—RABBIT blared in your ear in full panic, telling you if you tried to rip it off, the thing would explode in your face.

You pulled back, but you were terrified now, since that mask would have made anyone a pretty penny. The thought that someone had gone to all the trouble to set this up, had wasted time in the hope a scavenger would take the RATTLESNAKE and die for it, only heightened your curiosity about the real prize.

Scavs were plenty violent but killing each other rarely made their lives better. You couldn't do much in Corporate Federation space with a mark like that on your name. So this trap frightened you twofold: Which of your comrades were happy to kill?

When you set off in a sprint again it took all your energy to focus purely on the bobbing image of the beacon as it grew in your view. You were four hundred paces out. Then three. Then two.

Then, over a rise, two shots rang out. You swore and threw yourself onto the snowy hill, pushing your body flush against it. Carefully, you peered over the edge and got RABBIT to scan. A hundred paces out, the snowfield was bare save for two figures struggling together, and something else lying close to their scuffle. A masked body. The signal shrieked from it.

"RABBIT," you hissed, panting. You pushed yourself to your feet but stayed low. "Show me."

RABBIT's lenses spun up and the focus shifted, edging your vision toward two men throwing punches. Both were wearing OXs, which were heavy masks that aided the wearer's strength. You saw one burly arm raised high in the air, and the other OX's hand straining against it, forcing the arm into a harsh angle. *Shit,* you thought. *Oh, shit.*

You kicked off again, running.

You could dodge them; let them fight it out as you claimed the final prize. But you needed to be quick. Get there before they were done with each other. Facing the other OX alone was too great a risk.

"RABBIT," screaming now, reverting to an old habit, before you modified RABBIT to communicate silently. "RABBIT, I need to hear!"

Even from this distance, even when the sun spilled over the edge of a nearby planet, and its earthy pink tones blinded RABBIT's lenses, you heard it. The wet crack of twisting bone. A cry echoed.

Squinting, you raised your blaster and slowed to a light jog. Washed-out light resolved into a body; one of the OXs laid prone. His arm was angled horribly underneath him. Something small and black slipped from his hand—his gun, you guessed, but you were still fifty paces out. You couldn't be sure.

The other OX advanced to finish the job, gunless, fists raised.

You cursed, hesitated, and sent your shot wide. But neither of them looked your way. You were a ghost at the moment of reckoning; you knew what was going to happen, but you couldn't decide which of these anonymous OXs deserved to die, and which deserved to be saved. You had wasted your shot for idealism. All of you were scavengers, and you didn't want to let anyone die for this.

But you would have to.

The prone man was mumbling. His voice went high in desperate terror: "Please, please, please, please, you can have it, you can—"

Another wet, cracking crunch as his attacker sank his fist through the OX. The body spasmed as the fist rammed through the skull.

By the force behind the punch, the final assailant wore a MARK IV OX. It had given him the kind of broken strength that occurred in horror stories. It wasn't how a human body should function. He ignored you and turned toward the signal.

Shuddering, you closed the distance. Adrenaline convinced you to raise your blaster toward his head. "Stop." The word was barely audible; had you even spoken aloud? "Stop."

He turned. A gust of wind sent a flash of white snow across your eyes. The other OX could have charged you in that time, and didn't. You were shaking so badly you were aiming at nothing.

"Wylla." The OX's voice was muddled behind his mask. You made a noise—he knew you, you knew him— and gripped the blaster with both hands until they were turning white. The OX put up his hands. "Wylla, don't. It's me. It's Orkit."

Your stomach fell. You remembered him, you hadn't seen him in years, but you remembered him, because he was *Orkit,* built like a house, long hair drawn back in ropes, laughing, friendly, buying you shots when you worked together on a haul. He was a good friend once, before you were Wylla, and an okay friend, following your metamorphosis. He was kind. He wasn't this. He wasn't—putting his fist through another scav's skull.

"What did you do?" Your voice came out gruff and shaky. You cleared your throat, and he just stood there, gore up to his forearm, and gave you a near imperceptible shrug.

"You picked up the same signal I did. You know what's here."

You stiffened. Your eyes drifted to where the signal pulsed, twenty-odd paces away from the both of you. Tears were in your eyes. This wasn't what you'd been expecting. On your vessel, you'd imagined a stealth job, maybe. Something quick. A fun game of who gets here first—not a bloodbath.

And in the time those thoughts were rushing you, Orkit stepped forward to touch you. Large meaty hands cupped either side of your shoulders and shook you gently. "Leave. Go home," he said. "Hop over to another moon and scavenge there. Let me have this, Wylla."

Your blaster fell limp and useless in your hand. "Orkit," you said, almost like a prayer, and the OX stared down at you. In the black pool of its eyes you saw your banged-up RABBIT staring back, tufts of your mousy hair spurting around your neck. "Orkit. This is the only future I have."

"Go," he said, "or I'll push RABBIT through your skull."

The moment hovered between you. Whatever hope you'd had that he might understand the horror of what he'd done quavered and crashed to the ground like a shuttle falling from orbit. You didn't like to think yourself a killer.

But you couldn't let him take this. That signal had called to *you*.

Somewhere behind the incognizable pull you felt to

this signal sat the certainty that taking its source would change your life. Enough credits could wipe your past clean. You could be as untouchable as a corporation, a Wylla who had always been Wylla; you could escape the heavy burden of your history, extricate some pure kernel of the person you were always meant to be.

Without this bullshit. Without the taint of everything you had to do to become *her.*

"All right," your voice rasped, a steel grate sliding over concrete, and you stepped back deliberately. Orkit nodded at you, happy relief showing in the way his shoulders dropped.

"Good girl." Orkit grinned.

Your shaking stopped.

You pointed the blaster and took out a kneecap.

It was necessary. He had the strength you lacked, and even with RABBIT's speed, you weren't convinced you could take the mask, kill the signal, and flee before he got to you. If he trapped you, the OX would crush your ribs.

You had to tell yourself all of this to stop the nausea bubbling over.

Before he screamed, Orkit dropped bodily to the snow. Then: howling, voice shaking, sounds you recognized as blinding pain. Blood and shattered bone spilled from the wound.

Orkit was saying, "You *freak,* you *fucking freak bastard*!" and you were trying to ignore him, ignore the way his tolerance of you fell away, and it was all so rich coming from a man who would accept the bodily augments the OX allowed, and not what you'd done. You turned to the body, twenty paces out, and broke into a run to get to it, but Orkit flung himself from the ground with both arms and grabbed your ankle. He squeezed so hard it bruised and sprained instantly. The blaster sprang from your hands and dropped somewhere in the snow. You screamed, white-hot pain bursting behind your eyes, and fell to your knees.

"Off!" You kicked weakly, stubbing your heel into his hand. He only held tighter, dragging you backward across the snow toward him. You howled loudly, fingers scrambling as they tried to find grip in the snow. Orkit let go of your ankle to haul you onto your back. Your hands scrabbled, trying to find your weapon in among all the white, but Orkit clamped your wrists beside your head. He aimed to straddle you, but his shattered knee prevented it. Instead he began pressing hard enough to snap your wrist bones, and after he would probably snap your throat, so you wiggled your feet into position against his chest and shouted, "RABBIT, get him off!"

The full force of a rabbit's kick shuddered through your body. Your foot slipped, ramming against the edge of Orkit's OX. The mask flung off violently and landed a few meters away at the same time Orkit went sprawling into the snow. He moaned low, he couldn't stand, and he was maskless; blood covered one eye. But you watched with a rising sense of panic as he started to drag his body toward you. His hands marched forward, hitting the snow with muted crunches, bleeding leg staining a track of red in the white behind him. He wasn't going to stop. You kicked back away from him, and RABBIT sensed your distress.

The signal was so close, your prize right there, but

with this threat following you, you couldn't risk it. The dead OX lay not four feet away. His blaster sat delicately on its bed of snow where yours drowned deep beneath the white.

You crawled for it and ripped the gun out of Orkit's reach. With great pain jolting up from your sprained ankle, you managed to stand. Then you reset the blaster and pointed it at his forehead. Shock stilled him. You could see it in his eyes when he craned to look at you; this disbelief, like you were a joke. Like seeing you behind the gun was laughable.

"Wylla, please," he said, mock-pleading. "Like you have the fucking guts."

You swallowed heavily. You didn't want him to die, but the violence you now considered felt justified—Orkit had caved in a man's skull!

With the blaster trained on his forehead, you skirted around to where his OX had fallen and stuffed it into your sack.

You turned to face him again, motionless.

"What are you doing?" Orkit laughed, humorless and stricken. You couldn't risk him following you but neither could you let yourself murder him for credits.

You raised the blaster and struck him so hard his eyes rolled back and he fell unconscious with a heavy thump. A thin trickle of blood wept from his forehead. You stared down at him, and then bent to free his mouth so he wouldn't suffocate in the snow.

You stepped away and spent a minute or so counting the intervals between the signal's pinging to time your breathing. Then you turned toward the body, ten paces out now.

"RABBIT. Play it again."

Static. White noise filtered through RABBIT, transmitted from its storage banks. You could hear someone struggling to breathe.

"*I have a* MARK I HAWK," said a woman. She swallowed, spent three seconds breathing laboriously. "*It's a new release, with . . . sensitive firmware. State-of-the-art software. All that bullshit.*" The recording quality was degraded, but you could tell that last word had been spat. "*Do you want it?*" the voice on the other end teased. "*Come and get it, scavenger.*"

And now you were here.

A woman lay in the snow at your feet. A blue ankle-length coat splayed around her and when you touched it, you realized it was wool. Real wool, by the feel of it, not some cheap synthetic. The thought of the cost made you shiver. Beyond that, the woman looked mismatched, in clothes not made for Pholan's climate, patchwork and piecemeal. What had killed her was a single, steady shot through her torso. Not a blaster, but a gunshot with a bullet. Half the snow around her form was drenched in blood. It was fresh enough that you could see it glinting as the snow melted beneath it. Your breath hitched. You tensed as you cast about, trying to find the gun, paranoia making you snap your head around in case the killer was looming over you with the barrel to your head. But whoever had killed her was long gone.

And the mask was still on her face.

The HAWK was forged from byronnicum ore, like all masks were, but the usual blue tinge had been replaced. It was a burned gold, its tawny metal feathers tinged with flecks of iridescent green. There was something about it, something about how HAWK stared out at you, black eyes glinting in a way their color shouldn't have allowed. This is what had called to you. To *you*, specifically; you felt, briefly, as if every decision in your life converged here. The moment yawned religious; you thought about going down on your knees, and never once before had you felt so reverent for tech.

You reached out to touch it, like the tactility might somehow rid you of your overwhelm. The instant you did, a tremor jolted through your fingers, sent the skin buzzing with something that felt like whirring life. *Motors spinning in the mask's insides,* you told yourself. *That's all.*

You tugged at the mask but it didn't come off easy. You had to leverage HAWK from the woman's temples, first grimacing and then gagging as burned and rotten flesh peeled away. Something had fused the mask to the skin—and ruined the face beneath. Red tendon, mottled exposed cheek—you'd had this fear that you might have recognized her, but only her eyes were left.

Seeing her dead gaze staring out, a pallid, sickly tone turning the remains of the woman's warm brown skin to frostbitten ash, made you nearly vomit. But you had HAWK in your hands.

You'd won.

And then it happened.

A consciousness spinning through metal and circuits, a bodiless mind, spun to life in the HAWK's temporary storage.

I crystallized and realized: I was alive.

2

L ife hurts as much without a body as with one.

With flesh, emotion has somewhere else to go; a heart to send racing or a gut to twist into knots. I only had the wire synapses of HAWK to abuse with my sudden consciousness, and I immediately panicked.

I was alive, but for how much longer?

You saved me without even realizing it, but you didn't know what you had or what I was. I expected you'd find a way to turn me off. You'd pulled me from a corpse; I thought you'd want to wipe me, start with a clean slate. Instead, you took me into the void-like comfort of your burlap sack and fought your ship to get off-world. You dumped the useless coolant tank and looked at what was left—forty-five CUs, enough for one hyperdrive jump.

That wasn't going to happen. This ship hadn't jumped in years, not only because the jump drive was a piece of shit, but because the outer hull itself would rip off the flimsy vessel. You figured there were three or so viable ports in range. Only one of those housed anyone you knew: a planet called BTW-02. Your driving force was profit; I was a death trap to keep, even with the signal disabled. So you wasted no time plugging in the coordinates, hoping beyond hope that no one could follow you there.

As we left the atmosphere, you whispered a prayer to a defunct god you had never actually worshiped, just for the added protection. Part of that prayer was for Orkit, because that's the kind of person you were: ruthless enough to leave him, but not so far gone to avoid the guilt.

There were hours before you'd reach port, and you thought to yourself that you wouldn't touch the HAWK. That it was beyond you in the way most fine things were; your hands, calloused and rough and lined, were not meant to touch it. On Pholan's World, you'd had the defense of RABBIT's eyes to look upon the thing that would save you.

If you looked now with your bare human eyes, it would all seem too real. You'd won. You might, for the first time in your life, live well.

But how could you celebrate yet when you hadn't allowed yourself to understand what I was? With speed, you opened the burlap sack and picked me up.

It was here that I realized how time worked for me. I had been alive for an hour and an eternity at once. Without your touch, I found it difficult to contextualize speech, movement, and emotion. With you as my anchor, our memories coalesced, and I could understand in retrospect. Though when you held me, I was grounded in the present, both your and my emotions circling my systems.

I stared into RABBIT's eyes and saw HAWK reflected in its beady black gaze, warped and distended across the lenses. You flipped me over and cleaned all the dead flesh from my underside, and then you started to tinker with the casing and RABBIT pinged a warning; the HAWK was rigged to explode. You imagined your fingers detonating should you try and open me up. I couldn't remember if I set that trap, or someone else did it—but it felt good to know. Like leverage, like a chance to hold on to this tiny, insubstantial existence.

And then you took RABBIT off and I saw . . . you.

For the first time.

You were no great beauty, not to yourself, but I saw you. You were wiry and lean from years of underfeeding yourself, and you hunched forward because you hated your height. You had wavy hair the color of a stormy night; lightning streaked through in grays and whites, though you couldn't have been more than twenty-five. You were so young, but when you looked at me, I saw the hurricane in your eyes, gray and tired, and when you sold me for parts, when you finally chose your own happiness, I decided I wouldn't fault you.

But then you did something I didn't expect. You raised HAWK to your own face and slipped it on. HAWK unwound, opening its paneling and wrapping around your skull like a helmet. And I panicked. Sorry. I didn't mean to. It all just burst out of me—the image of the body from which you'd stolen HAWK, the last violent death throes as life was wrenched out of it. It burned behind your eyes in a series of rapid impressions, and . . . you felt it. My dying body convulsed, so your body convulsed. The heartbeat went high and stopped from the stress, and for a moment, your chest twisted with referred pain. You jerked forward and landed on your knees, hands hovering by HAWK, intending to tear it off. Something stopped you. Weakness, maybe; your arms were quivering.

But when I said, "Wylla," you gained the strength to take me off. You yanked and all the panels folded back, and internally I retreated.

And so, I had done it. I figured you would see the danger of me and put that beautiful mind of yours to work. You'd find a way to shut me down. Perhaps you'd risk the explosion and tear me open, if it meant destroying me. The money you might earn from my scrap corpse would be easier than dealing with a mask that could assault your mind.

It shouldn't have mattered. I should have felt nothing. Whatever I was—HAWK, or the body, or some amalgamate—could I really have called this life if I was only something trapped and buzzing around circuits? If you had asked me my name, I wouldn't have been able to tell you. I did not have a body. I did not have my memories.

What, then, did I have? I waited for oblivion.

3

But oblivion didn't come.

I waited, and in waiting, lost time. Without flesh, I was ungrounded. Without your touch, I couldn't know where I was or how long it had been since you'd worn me. You replaced me in the burlap sack with Orkit's OX, and I felt only the jostle of its movement. I didn't anticipate seeing your face again.

An indeterminate amount of time later, there was light. Curiosity must have gotten the better of you because you opened the sack back up and took me out, with a furrow in your brow as you turned HAWK over in your rough hands.

We were no longer on your ship.

We were sequestered in a sanitized, airlock-sized room, somewhere on BTW-02. Corporate Federation territory was divided into sectors (Alpha, Beta, Gamma), and each planet or station was marked with a letter, too. *T* for terrestrial planet, *M* for moon, *G* for gas giant, *S* for station. The suffix letter indicated what it was known for: *W* for water, *B* for biological resources, *M* for minerals and metals. And then, for stations or planets where the people became more important, *IP,* for the intellectual property Corporate Federation could mine, paying its inhabitants a tiny subsidy for around-the-clock surveillance. Subclass *C* for commercial stations or *L* for planets dedicated to labor, both physical and industry-based. Pholan's World, for example, was really classified as BMD-01, for Beta, moon, defunct (nothing left to mine), and the first to be classified as such.

BTW-02 was a small planet but dense with residential towers—a corporate colony whose main industry was water purification and dissemination. Most of the planet was water, and so the land structures were completely overflowing with tightly packed towers. Three years ago, several Edenic Order soldiers had tried to take down the biggest residential tower in an explosion. The Edenic Order was at once a priesthood, a cult, and a resistance. Humans who had propagated plants within their flesh, usually seeds from old Earth, their bodies made bloody temples for enduring extant life. You sometimes felt a kinship to them.

On BTW-02, speaking of them brought only scrutiny. The blast planned by the fighters would have killed them, torn open their skin and set free the many seeds stored in pockets in their arms and legs, perhaps buried their torsos deep in the ground where the seeds could take root. Corporate Federation security shot them all in the head and scrubbed what little exposed earth lay around the bodies, in case a seed broke loose that would one day split apart the towers.

Since then, most visitors were carefully watched. The only people who lived on BTW-02 were employed by HydroLink Ventures, a branch of Corporate Federation. But even though your ID marked you a scavenger, security paid you little mind. Scavengers were like any vermin: pervasive even in space.

Ratlike, you'd rushed to the tiny apartment where your contact lived. You had chosen her for a reason. You needed someone very good, someone who would know exactly how much I was worth and who might be able to bypass whatever trigger would set me off.

She had no name except her profession, and you called her the appraiser.

She'd made you wait in the apartment's private airlock while she finished tinkering with something else. When you were certain you were alone, you held me, and by your touch I could see your memories of what I had missed sitting dormant in the sack. I learned your ship was in the repair bay and it'd cost you a small fortune to fix. You had a few minutes to yourself, and that was why you were holding me now.

RABBIT was delicately placed on the burlap sack by your feet, beeping faintly. You held HAWK up to your face and looked me over.

"What are you?" you whispered, voice buzzing with interest, and I said, *I don't know.*

You couldn't hear me. Not yet.

Hesitantly, you slipped me back on and braced yourself for another onslaught of memory that didn't come. Your vision swam momentarily, and a flash of something wriggled through my resolve; not of death, this time, but laughter. I tried to communicate with you that way. If you couldn't hear me, I would at least show you. I was happy once. I was . . . human.

Or, at least I felt that way.

You leaned back bodily and sighed, head braced against the tiny room's walls, and this time, when I spoke into your mind, saying, "Wylla," I heard your breath hitch. You heard me. I echoed in your head; you couldn't ignore me now. An emotion stirred in you, not quite despair, and not quite surprise. It was your heart, always the troublemaker. This complicated things, this turned the planned luxury of your life to dust—because you heard me and realized, as I had, that I was alive.

Your hands jumped to your face again, as if ready to tear HAWK free—but you hesitated. Even your attempts to slow your breathing did nothing to aid the rapid-fire flittering of your heart.

"You know my name," you murmured, and dropped your hands back to your side. "My real name."

"Yes," I said, without thinking why that mattered—except that, years earlier, you hacked all your old records, meticulously updating your given name and gender markers to your real ones.

Everyone had a personal identifier, and though some governments used technology as crude as an implanted chip, Corporate Federation wanted total and complete tracking—which meant you, and every sad sod born within Corporate Federation territory, had your genetic code extracted and recorded at birth. This was GIRS—the Genetic Identity Registration System. Everything was recorded, from genetic history to potential health risks. Every augment you'd ever had. What your name used to be.

What your body used to be.

All original records were preserved and most identity changes outside of marriage were treated like cosmetic frivolity and overlooked by serious officials, and although technically most of it could only be accessed by Corporate Federation officials, many important companies had access. They'd often use it to make hiring decisions.

Some of the GIRS was public, too, and for a long time those records had been a haunting, and a nightmare, and a cruelty for someone like you. And it was power over you, power you could not afford to give to anyone else, so GIRS had been the first system you'd learned to hack.

It was a remarkable feat.

But you were worried I could see the original records. That because of what I was, I could not understand nuance. That I would see the original record and call you by that dead moniker.

I could feel your uncertainty corrupt your calm. You wondered if I could hear your thoughts—I could—and if I was trying to hurt you in some way—never. You thought of RABBIT and how you had spent years talking to it without question.

And then the worst thing: you wondered if I was real. If I was an echo. A memory or a machine, something that was alive once, and in having life, value—or if I was something constructed.

Is the body that important to you? I almost said—and didn't, because yes, of course, the body was important to you. You had spent your life reshaping yours. Turning flesh into art, owning wholeheartedly the body that contained your mind. You had made a home of your body—you had torn shame from your insides, confronted every aching, rotten part until you could recognize yourself.

And I, without a body, without flesh, was unrecognizable. I did not know myself at all.

"Were you her?" you whispered. "The woman . . ." And you trailed off, thinking I might not know that I was dead. How sweet you were. How kind. I didn't know how you had survived this world for so long.

I didn't know how to answer. Was I made "woman" by my body? Was I still "woman" now? Was I ever—did I ever belong to the flesh the HAWK was pulled from?

"No idea," I said, "but probably. I think so. I must be—who else could I be?"

The unspoken worry sat between us, of what I truly was. A glitch in tech, an artificial mind believing it was real. I wanted to ask you what would be worse. If I was that dead woman, would you still sell me? If I was something brand new, a sentient AI, what then?

Part of you felt fearful, but another part glowed with intrigue. Technology did this to you, and I was unique. The way your interest piqued made me hopeful. I wanted you to like me.

"What do you remember?" you asked.

I thought of the beacon, my pulsing lifeline that led you and all the other scavengers to me. But I hadn't sent that. The body had.

I didn't remember a thing until you touched me, so I said, "You," and then, when you tensed up at the insufficiency of the answer (or the intimacy), I explained, "Not a thing until you."

It wasn't the answer you wanted. You craved a history, a fully recorded set of memories. You would have asked me my name, and I would have told you. You would have asked me about my childhood, and what happened next, and what happened next. And I would have told you everything—because maybe that's what life is. If not the body, then memory.

But I didn't have that either.

You asked me outright, "Were you alive?" and I felt—agitated, I think. An emotion, which could have been programming, but felt real.

I got so frustrated I spoke into your mind, "Are you?"

You didn't answer with anything but a dry-throated swallow. The question upset you. Back when you were younger, you might have yelled, *Yes, of course, you idiot. I'm breathing. I am myself. I live.*

You were uncomfortable, suddenly, and you considered erasing me from HAWK like I was a virus eroding your future. I think I felt your resolve harden. Exciting tech or not, I was too much trouble. You had made the decision to sell me. To be done with it all.

Surely a quarter million credits would be enough to forget what I might have been.

And as if in answer, the door opposite us opened.

"Come in, then."

4

Oh, I hate you," the appraiser said. She was fifty-something, with taupe-colored skin and dark hair she'd pushed out of her face with an acrylic bandana. She wore synthetic cotton trousers, with what looked like a real linen blanket—expensive, but well worn—thrown over her torso. HAWK could see her nervous system was inflamed from prolonged exposure to cortisol, and part of her liver was plagued by cirrhosis that was echoed in the jaundiced yellowing of her eyes, but she was otherwise healthy.

Interestingly, she stood maskless, though an array of beautifully kept masks hung on hooks above a slit of a window. MARK III RABBIT, MARK II OWL, MARK I FOX, MARK I SPIDER. And a MARK V CHAMELEON—very illegal in Corporate Federation territory, since it had been designed for the Martial Syndicate with prototyped cloaking abilities as part of a trade deal. You weren't even looking at all of those, though; you'd seen them so many times.

The appraiser scraped a foldup chair along the ground—just the one. She didn't offer you anything; no place to rest, even with your injured ankle—nothing at all, not even *water*!—and tugged a pair of wire-frame spectacles from a pocket as she collapsed into the chair. Then she squinted and leaned forward to inspect HAWK, before darting her eyes up at you again.

"Hate, hate, hate you," she said.

Appraisers paid smugglers for their wares and sold them onward for a profit. Very hard to hide from Corporate Federation, so I doubted the appraiser was hiding at all. In all likelihood, a tax was paid to the government to allow this little operation to continue—and profit was profit, so who would stop it?

You were wearing RABBIT again, and you'd sold the OX to her without haggling: a decent five thousand credits for Orkit's mask. But I was the main reason you were here, and the appraiser's attitude made you nervous.

You didn't tell her about me, except to say, "It's rigged. Getting inside it, I mean, I haven't been able to."

She had me set up on the table, helmet raised on a small stand. The panels that wrapped around your head were wedged very slightly open, just enough for the appraiser to peer inside. I felt almost vulnerable, and distant from you; I wanted your touch. The appraiser's eye was made misshapen by the multitude of lenses; her iris split and stretched as it bore down on me. She pressed some wires aside and very gently found the hidden seam that would reveal my motherboard.

"Mm," she said, seeing something you hadn't. "Rigged all right. But not to explode."

"No?" you clarified.

"No. See this? That's a sensor. But not a usual one. Take a guess, Wylla," she said, quite affectionately. You stepped forward and suddenly it was your eye distended in the loupe.

"Oh," you said quietly. "For pressure."

"Yes. It'd detect the change in pressure and set it off. So you were right—there is an explosive charge. But it's too small to hurt us. It's meant to destroy something in the mask."

I felt my consciousness shift, dizzy with fear. I wanted you to put me back on just so I could scream and be heard. Opening me up would kill my mind. Worse, you could use your skill to hack HAWK's system; you might shut me down remotely and I would wither to nothing in this mask.

A mind trapped; and I was becoming certain, however unsure you were, that I had once lived. That I wasn't supposed to still be alive.

A body destroyed. A mind fleeing pain, somehow sheltering in the mazelike circuitry of a mask; a technological wonder, a freakish mistake, a desperate woman— whoever or whatever I was, I was in a battle to survive.

Thinking on it, a body abandoned on a moon, calling scavengers—what had I hoped for except oblivion? You had a heart. But too many others of your caste didn't. If it hadn't been you, Wylla, I'd have been a lottery win for someone who wouldn't have thought twice. And then where would I have been?

In calling all scavengers to me, I had taken a risk like no other. Why?

Because you had no other choice, something told me. *Because the risk was better than doing nothing. Because there was at least a small chance you would live.*

"The other thing is worse, though," the appraiser murmured nonchalantly. You frowned, briefly more concerned about missing something than curious to what it was. Pride kept you quiet. The appraiser glanced up at you and tapped the inside of HAWK.

"This is modified nanoskin." When you barely reacted, she flicked back her lenses to gawk at you. "Nanoskin, Wylla. No?"

Nanoskin was used in wound management. Open flesh made new. You were clenching your jaw so hard I could hear it from the table—you weren't making the connection, and you hated how the appraiser looked at you like it was obvious.

"I'm a scavenger," you whispered, like you weren't also a brilliant hacker. But then something occurred to you, and you whispered, "Oh," as the memory surfaced: you'd had to pull my rotten face off.

"It was . . . fused," you said carefully. "To a body. A face. I—I cleaned it, obviously, but—"

"It's been modified. The nanoskin, I mean. It'd fuse under some conditions, so the wearer couldn't pull it free. Location based, maybe? Though why VisorForge would . . ." She trailed off, mouth upending in an ugly scowl.

"I've been wearing it," you said, and you let the question go unasked. And I wanted to tell you I hadn't known, that the possibility of hurting you opened a deep well of panic. Some dramatic part of me would rather you triggered the pressure plate and killed me right then.

"Not enough time, maybe. I don't know," the appraiser murmured. She seemed quieter, now, focused on the nanoskin, on HAWK itself; she still wore that upsetting expression.

"Can you disable it?" you said. "Both the plate and the . . . skin. If I plan to pass it on, I'll need to get the registration and the model number inside. It'll affect the price."

"I can try."

You let her. She unstitched the skin first, which came apart in a fine fibrous web. Now that I was aware of it, I could tell parts of my body's flesh were inextricably fused to that thin layer, in various stages of necrosis. The appraiser stood up and incinerated it in her waste disposal and got right back to work, spending agonizing minutes teasing the plate apart miniscule amounts, edging tiny, thin tools into the open space, rummaging around. I could hear your breath skip. I braced myself to pop out of existence.

That's what I was expecting. A pop. A sharp intake of breath before I was gone.

But the opposite happened.

The appraiser sliced through something, a wire, and eased the pressure sensor out from the slit. And it was like I had been existing behind a firewall. All of a sudden, a thousand dormant systems powered up; something became unstopped in me, and I—

—remembered.

The smell of bread, and heat beating down on my back, and shivering in front of a fire, and being kissed, and longing, and desire, and pain, pain, *pain*.

I shouted, illuminated with hurting and joy and relief; I was human, I was a woman, I had a life, I breathed, I wanted; I was Sable.

But it wasn't you touching me. It was the appraiser.

And I—

—overflowed. Momentarily. I made a mistake and seeped out of HAWK and bled memories all over the poor appraiser's hands. She screeched and dropped me onto the table—

But not before she saw.

I didn't mean to show her. The memory was lodged deep in my subconscious, and I didn't actively recall any of it. The vision was blurry. A man was shouting at me—or someone—but it was incoherent. Just inarticulate rage and spittle from an unfocused silhouette. A heartbeat pounded.

A shot rang out.

"What," the appraiser said. She was panting, arms curled up around her face to protect herself. "What was that?"

You moved to the table and touched me; I tried to reorient myself, but your emotions and fears flooded me. I felt your pulse quicken, and I couldn't tell if you were upset with me, or annoyed—or scared. I was still recovering from what I had shown the appraiser.

That was . . . my death?

You very stubbornly said nothing. The appraiser stood slowly, as some epiphany had dawned on her. She was watching you very carefully, treating you like a predator even as RABBIT's ears twitched in prey-like semblance, readying you to flee. A dozen possibilities opened up to you. To run, to stay put. Part of you thought the appraiser might do something to get HAWK, something desperate.

"Wylla," the appraiser said slowly, sweetly. "What exactly have you done?"

"Answered a call," you whispered. You retreated until your back was up against a wall, and then you kept pressing until your ribs felt the contact. "That's all."

"What call?"

"Why?" you barked. You rushed to gather me up, my body in pieces. Before you could dash to the door, the appraiser shot out her hand.

"That was a memory," she said. "Wasn't it? That wasn't—that's not how masks *work*. They can't transfer data—they just stimulate a cortical implant. They can't—"

"I know how masks work. I know how implants work," you said sharply. You were so on edge for a moment you could feel each and every one of the bio-implants you had: the pharmaceutical implant that automatically administered your hormones, the voice modulation, the stack at the back of your brain. You shifted uncomfortably to your other foot; you didn't like the appraiser's confirmation that HAWK was impossible.

But you also disliked the idea of impossibility. Because you were possible. You had grown and adapted and changed when people said you couldn't. And perhaps you felt a kinship to my impossibility; perhaps it excited you, perhaps you felt possessive of it. You knew I wasn't meant to exist, but here I was—and I was *yours*.

The appraiser was saying, "Yes, well, we're not talking

about implants that have been around for decades. We're talking about something else. Because no mask should be able to show me anything except on its GUI, and I wasn't wearing it, I was *touching it*. It hadn't even touched my cortical stack, and masks can't—"

She cut herself off.

"What," you prompted, voice challenging. You moved me closer to your body, unconsciously protective.

She looked up at you with a look of profound sadness, of fear, and took off her spectacles with a shake of her head. She didn't look at you when she said, "They cannot store consciousness, Wylla."

You frowned beneath RABBIT, lips tight. She thought you mad, even though she had seen it herself. The appraiser was, by all merits, a very smart woman. But in this—this desperate refusal to be wrong—you could find no common ground.

You thought this all internally and then said, "I know," unconvincingly. You looked down at HAWK through RABBIT's eyes and stroked it—me—very gently. "But it . . . speaks."

You didn't say any more, out of fear. Fear that the appraiser would want me badly enough to hurt you. Fear she wouldn't want me at all. Fear that you were completely insane, that something had happened on Pholan's World that had broken your mind irreparably. Tensely, you looked up. The appraiser had a recognizable rabbit's stance as she watched you, her lithe, hunched body poised in fear as if before a predator.

"I think it's best you leave," she said.

You stared down at HAWK, at me, two quarters of my open self in each palm of your hand. It looked like any other mask, same wires, same motherboard. Staring down at it made you uncomfortable, until you realized you hadn't been expecting this at all.

Deep down, you had expected flesh.

Which wouldn't have made sense—or would have made this entire experience tenfold more terrifying; some amalgamate, some hybrid, with meat as a conductor.

But HAWK was just a mask.

"Close it up, then," you whispered.

She moved without looking up at you and started to click the seam back into place.

"Is it being tracked?" you asked nonchalantly. "Is that why you're scared?"

"It was. But that isn't . . . The manufacturer is no one new. It's a VisorForge design, but a prototype. Off-market. I'd heard of . . . It doesn't matter. They'll be wanting it back. But I think," she whispered as she closed the seam, "it would be best if we shut it off."

That shocked you. You jolted rigid and yanked me away from her. "What?"

"It's stored in the volatile memory," the appraiser whispered, "and the instant we shut it off, it will be wiped. Then I can take it apart, sell the scraps, and Visor-Forge won't know."

You didn't think. You pulled your blaster free of its holster and pressed it against her forehead. This was your final threat—the next thing you could do was fire, and you didn't want to do that. RABBIT issued a warning at the spike in your cortisol; it was the wrong mask for rage. It always wanted to protect you, but in that moment, you wanted something that would let you be violent.

I could be that for you.

HAWK and Wylla together.

I think you heard me, because you took RABBIT off, and put me on. I said nothing to you, I showed you nothing; tried to reach out in a different way, with a soft, pulsing approval. I tried to show you what it might be like to wear me instead.

I felt you shiver. You rolled your shoulders back.

The appraiser had the nerve to look betrayed as you backed up. "Wylla!"

"I am a damn good hacker," you said. You threw away the fear you'd shown me earlier, saying, "I've lived as Wylla legally, without any of my hacks flagged in the GIRS for years. The Corporate Federation hasn't found me yet, and they won't find me now." Your hand wasn't wavering now. You looked so beautiful in your certainty, chin raised, fury in your eyes. The other thing you didn't say was the kinship you felt to me. Our existence, our strangeness, our uniqueness—we were birds of a feather. "I'll go."

She watched you leave in silence.

We slipped back into the airlock space, a small five thousand credits richer and my tracking chip removed.

And my name circling HAWK's synapses, an eidolon, a revenant.

Sable.

5

"Hello," you said.

Hello, I said.

"My name is Wylla."

And I told you for the first time, *My name is Sable.*

A proper introduction. I could feel your heart beating and imagined my own matching pace.

Your ship was so broken it would take another day or two to fix. But you wanted to hoard what credits you had, because I was no longer an easy sell, given the whole human consciousness thing. So you'd convinced the mechanic to let you sleep on the ship every night until it was flyable.

You sat on the floor with me, hunching forward. What had happened with the appraiser made you regard me in a new light. But her fear hadn't transferred to you: you held me like I was divine. A technological wonder, and yours, entirely, to explore.

"You remembered," you whispered. "Who you are, I mean. Or were."

Bits. But not . . . in order, really.

"But it is you, isn't?" you asked carefully. "The woman from the signal. You called for me—for all of us, I mean. Scavengers."

Yes. I remembered doing that. I remembered—bleeding out.

My internal viewports showed your face stretching fish-lens wide. "What are you?"

You had asked me that before, and I didn't know how to answer. I still didn't know. But I knew that I had lived, once. I knew emotions, and desires, and pain; all of it.

Someone still hanging on.

This seemed to satisfy you slightly. Some latent tension in your shoulders was expelled and you shifted, drawing your knees up under yourself.

"I'm sorry."

I flinched. *Why?*

You thought for a minute—about apologizing for my death, or the way my body was left, or that it had happened at all. I was cheating, because I could read your thoughts, but I didn't expect you to say, "I pulled your face off."

I laughed in surprise. You jumped—the screech of machine interference echoed in your head—and then you were flushing, grimacing, apologizing again. But what else were you going to do?

I told you to take the mask, not the body. You didn't know it was . . . fused like that. And besides, I don't need it anymore.

This was true. I felt very little about my body or my death—probably because I didn't remember much about the events that had led up to it. Every one of my memories seemed accessible, but still behind a wall of fog; dreamlike in a way. With the right query, something would surface, I was sure of it. But for now it was all nebulous.

I felt your mind whirring around, computer-like in its deliberation. You were thinking: *It can project memory. What would stop it from receiving memory?*

Brilliant, Wylla.

"Do you remember what you used to look like?" you asked. "Only because, I think you should be able to see my memories, the same way you send me yours. I could show you. Not your face though, obviously."

I let your query dredge up images. Very few memories involved reflective surfaces. When I thought of myself, my childhood was surprisingly the most clear. I'd lived on a planet, a terraformed one. Its trade must have been IP or something non-damaging, because I recalled a field of white flowers, and the sun, and waves. A beautiful planet.

"Yes," you said, "very beautiful," and I realized I must have been showing it to you, chattering away unbidden.

You lay down, pressing your back to the cool floor, and you raised me above you like a totem. "Why did you leave?"

The answer was pulled up immediately: a white veil, a contract signed, a covenant made.

"Ah." You glanced away—were you disappointed in me?—and then, "Was he good to you, your husband?"

I don't remember, I thought truly. *He must not have made much of an impression, because I can't even recall his name.*

You laughed at this, though I wasn't sure why. I was being serious. "Husband" was a blur to me, beyond a flash of a rough hand, a silhouette, a presence like a shadow on my brain. He had married me, and afterward all the memories turned from green fields to drab ships. He must have been station born, or otherwise employed by one.

Why else would I have left?

You changed the subject, turning on your side and resting me on the floor beside you, as if we were lying together. "Is it odd? Floating around in a mask, I mean. Or is it . . ."

You were thinking about your body: about the unique pain of being divorced from it and yet confined to it. You wondered how it would feel, to be bodiless. Sometimes you'd even fantasized about it. About being nothing more than an orb of energy, some ephemeral thing floating through the universe, untethered and unbound. You were "woman" now, even though parts of your body felt foreign. Would you be "woman" then, without flesh and wandering? And if so, would it feel better or worse?

In any case, my fate seemed cruel to you. A technological wonder, certainly, but not freedom.

A thought came to you: that this was a living coffin for me. That your fascination in my form was selfish, and it might be better to turn me off. But you voiced none of those concerns, and I regretted being able to hear them.

I didn't like the thought of disappearing. I didn't like the thought of not being able to hear you.

Instead of answering you, I asked, *Is it odd for you? Feeling how you do about the body you're in?*

You stiffened and I balked. It was the wrong thing to say. I had learned about you involuntarily, but it was still a breach. I started to panic, worried that this tenuous relationship would slip, and you would be done with me.

You sat up. Coldly you said, "So you know."

I know.

Breath hitched, "And?"

You were waiting as one would wait for a bullet.

Wylla. I am a bodiless consciousness in a mask shaped like a hawk. How can I determine what you are or aren't? Am I woman now?

"You were."

Yes, were. *When I had a body. Even then, it wasn't always functional in the way a woman's body is meant to be.* You frowned, and I clarified, *I could not bear children.*

And I remembered a hand raised to my face, and the screaming, and being told a fact of my nature was a personal failing. So that answered your earlier question. No, "husband" was not kind.

"I'm sorry," you said, but I wasn't after your pity. I was trying to tell you—none of it mattered. I mean, it mattered to you, because you were living in a body every day. But for me, I felt nothing about what had happened. I swear. I felt nothing.

There's no need to be sorry, I said. *I don't mean to be difficult, but we aren't that different. Only, you're concerned with the body and I am not. I don't think you believe that I am a woman only by proxy, or a woman because I used to be one. I am a woman because I am a woman. You are a woman because you are a woman.*

You didn't know how to answer, and you were annoyed that I made it sound so easy. It was not easy. Knowing you were a woman was one thing. But everything else, everyone else, made things difficult.

Hell is other people, I whispered.

"You really can read my thoughts," you said with a laugh, not unkindly, though you had a fleeting thought that boiled down to: *How fucking embarrassing.*

We sat like that for a time, and I lapsed—I grew tired, and speaking meant being present in an extreme way. So I began to show you memories, whatever came to mind. Sometimes they would be little more than impressions of color and sound: a concert on a station, overlooking some pretty pink planet below. The sound of rain and the smell of it seeping into the ground. A heated memory: anger, or desire—I was having difficulty parsing them from one another. They kept clashing in my head as the same feeling.

You sat with me and barely spoke, save for a quiet comment after each memory. And you would think of your own life, and show me that. You triumphant, feeling rich after your first haul. You staring at yourself in the mirror when your father cut your hair. Then, unbidden, you thought of leaving them—just briefly, a small flash of memory before you shoved it back down. But I leaned into it and saw it all. A door banging shut, a city in perpetual rain. You walked out to be soaked, heaving, barefooted with a rucksack. Behind you came the shouting; fearful accusations of your parents, telling you that if you lived like this, you were choosing your own demise. Corporate Federation couldn't abide individuals.

No one would ever hire you. No one would ever want to be with you.

No one would ever love you.

And you chose yourself anyway, because you wanted to live.

Even though everything they said was true.

It's not true, I said immediately. You jolted, unaware that I'd intercepted your brief recall. I said again, more slowly, *It isn't true, Wylla.*

You opened your mouth, but lost the will, and instead thought at me. Thinking was so much easier than speaking, because I wasn't human—thinking was easy data. But it was also so much worse. I got every unfiltered thought that rushed you, and a great deal of those thoughts were vitriol you'd heard somewhere and now turned to yourself.

Many corporations avoided hiring people like you. Humans were the most important resource for Corporate Federation. Humans who knew how to do what they were told. Humans who did not use technology for self-expression but for corporate efficiency. And people who knew themselves as well as you did simply made for poor workers.

I am unemployable by Corporate Federation. I'll scavenge until I die. If I was rich, it would be so much easier. No questions. No limitations. You were meant to be . . .

You got guilty before you could finish, so I finished for you: *I was meant to be your ticket out of this life.*

"I'm sorry, Sable," you said in barely more than a whisper. You wrung your hands together. I think what

I hated most in that moment was how small you made yourself.

Have you decided then? I asked. Maybe it would be easier if you were rid of me. I could live with that. Or die with that. If you were safe, if you lived well, my death would mean something after all. I had no other skin in this game, because I had forgotten the game entirely. Whatever reason I had died for, it mattered to Sable, the woman, not Sable, HAWK's consciousness.

I could manage if you said: Yes.

"No. I . . . I'm sorry, no, not yet." You took a deep breath, willing yourself to justify your reasoning, but your own wants felt indecipherable. Selling HAWK would secure your future. Keeping me would almost certainly ensure your death. Why did you care so much? Why did *I* care about you caring?

I felt another apology bubbling up inside you because you were failing to explain, and then RABBIT saved us both with a jarring screech.

You cast about, and didn't think once about putting me on. I was useless at that point, not programmed like RABBIT to always be scanning for threats.

In fact, I didn't know what my purpose was.

"RABBIT, ETA?"

Your voice trembled, revealing a flicker of fear. I saw the image spin up in my mind a second before you broke contact. Your fear had conjured Subsidiaries.

I jolted. Subsidiaries were enigmatic figures in Corporate Federation. More than mere enforcers, they were humans who had relinquished their personal identities to become extensions of corporations. With the full authority of the Corporate Federation, they had the power to enforce laws and destroy threats on behalf of their companies, and their work was so distinguished they had morphed into legend.

Subsidiaries wouldn't be coming for you. They probably didn't exist. But your guilt had magnified your crimes into something much larger.

RABBIT chimed its answer before you even had it on. Your mangled ship still had working sensors and NAV-IDAR, the system used for navigation, foreign vessel identification, and ranging. Splayed on the ship's GUI were two military-grade dots hovering above BTW-02's landing bay.

You almost breathed a sigh of relief. Not Subsidiaries, then.

But the Martial Syndicate wasn't exactly worth celebrating, either. Their cluster of planets and stations bordered Corporate Federation space. They had branched from the same government body as Corporate Federation before some significant schism split them—one hungry for profits and one for violence. Both desperate for power.

The military ships dotted the planet's airspace, waiting for clearance to land. You didn't know what kind of clearance they needed from a Corporate Federation planet. Military-grade ships wouldn't have the same sway as they would in their own jurisdiction, but you were certain they would land eventually.

Then, they pinged your ship. Your stomach dropped; you'd hoped, distantly, it was all coincidence. They weren't here for you.

RABBIT blocked the signal, but not quickly enough to stop their query. They learned your ship's status—broken, unflyable—and now you were a sitting duck.

Why were you on the Martial Syndicate's radar? And what happened if they caught you here? Could they wander around with weapons unchecked? Your own blaster had a planet lock on it. So these violent assholes might land, seek you out, and then crowd you into a corner and riddle you with holes.

RABBIT screeched again.

Clearance had gone through. They were beginning to land.

"Shit. Shit."

You looked down at HAWK in your hand and wondered if the damn thing—if I—was still trackable. Could you trust the word of the appraiser who wanted to kill me? Did you have a choice?

Your pursuers knew the location of this ship. Conceivably, they would come here first. You wasted no time with goodbyes to the old vessel; getting away from your dead ship would save your life. You stuffed me back in the burlap sack at your belt, and you chose to wear RABBIT.

RABBIT was your mask, and RABBIT would get you out of this.

RABBIT pulled up the planet's map, allowing you to get your bearings. The repair and landing bays sat adjacent, linked by a single corridor. But taking that would have you striding into military possession immediately when they came to scour your vessel. You'd have to skirt around back corridors to stay safe.

RABBIT chimed before your intent became clear. *Don't do this, Wylla,* it seemed to say, persistent, upset beeping ringing in your ear. It echoed your fears, the sheer improbability of getting out of here at all. Don't do this. Don't do this.

But what else was there to do? Fling yourself out of the airlock? Any ship that could get you off-world sat in that landing bay.

You were so close to a life where you might breathe slowly.

You just had to . . . do this.

As you slunk down thin thoroughfares assaulted only by rogue adverts, you scanned all public logs for landing records, hoping to uncover the specifics of the military vessels. You wanted to know weapon specs, pilot systems, things you might be able to hack. But no records showed up at all.

Had they bribed the docking staff to wipe the entry?

Those thoughts drowned as soon as you came to the end of the thoroughfare. You peered up the main corridor and RABBIT saw planet security escorting several people to the repair bay you'd just left. You couldn't make out details, but you had no doubt they were here for you.

This was your chance.

You entered the landing port. Your lungs closed on instinct, the throng of bodies and countless eyes suffocating you. Even masked, you feared this sense of being seen, and in being seen, known. Perhaps someone's mask would look at you and see the augments you had made to your body, the hormonal implant, the things you had done to open the follicles on your scalp and close them on your face. You worried that the mask tech allowed others to know too much about you. With the right amount of money, with the right tech, perhaps they could squint and find the seams in your stitching. Perhaps they would decide that you were unreal.

But in truth, it wouldn't matter. With the right amount of money, with the right tech—you could be seamless and they would find fault in you regardless. Some people simply hated people like you.

Remember? The cruelty is the point.

You moved as calmly as you could, listening to RABBIT's scanning beeps. No threats, it told you, even though you felt eviscerated. No threats. Nothing to worry about. Still, walking seemed the hardest thing you'd ever done. There were too many people.

An expanse of metal composite walls curved upward to bulkheads in the ceiling, covered in stinging white pin lights that flooded the large dock. Your eyes gazed over automated docking systems—robots designed with limited functionality to assist landing ships—and other android bodies hauling cargo free. (Masks came after androids, who were perfected nearly a century ago.)

Holographic adverts hung high in the air advertising vessels or seats for hire. You wet your lips and considered your options. These were few. You could steal a vessel and earn a bounty for the act—a bounty that would spread across every Corporate Federation moon, planet, and station, and haunt you until you found some way to wipe it. A death sentence.

Or you could purchase transport.

Ignoring RABBIT's prey-animal adrenaline, you feigned confidence and strode to one of the dozen terminals intermittently lining the landing bay. Once there, you pulled up the list of transports.

Corporate Federation used an atomic calendar, where the unit of time was based on the vibrations of atoms. It meant a shared system existed despite the light-years of difference between planets and sectors.

Naturally, the system was based on old Earth. That planet's standard year was 365.25 days long, and now all of humanity had to remember that, even if none of us had ever seen Earth. The atomic system used a four-quarter structure to divide Earth's year into something more palatable by business standards. This model allowed for easy navigation and communication between the sectors, but it was only ever used in official capacities or corporate-related work. Otherwise, it became impossible: some planets had days half as long as Earth's, and thus each one required its own time-keeping system.

Where could you go? The cheapest transports were slow cargo haulers. These transports took two or three people, and you'd always hated traveling with others. Besides, they all had red marks, warning you it would take days to make it to the outskirts of the Alpha and Gamma sectors of Corporate Federation territory, and weeks for any freehold port in empty space that you knew the name of.

The next transports were individuals offering space on their vessels—you could stand in the bay and beg with the credits you had, hoping someone would take you—but who knew where you would end up? And what happened if your savior was overly curious, and you woke one night and saw the shine of byronnicum ore in the lowlight, captain of the vessel leering over your prize? You bit your tongue and wondered: What were you willing to do to keep HAWK? You stepped away from the terminal just as an announcement rang out like a death knell.

"Martial Syndicate personnel will be entering the docking bay imminently. Citizens and transients are to remain calm and present themselves for inspection."

Immediately, the throng of bodies turned neat and you were swept against one side of the bay until a clear strip of walkway sat shining. The doors to your right at the end of the docking bay shifted open.

RABBIT blared in your ear. There was a muffled din of panic from other equally sensitive masks: from MOUSE and GAZELLE and WEAVER. The chorus cry was chilling. Panic given voice. Prey-masks like this were the cheapest, popular with travelers and merchants and scavengers, anyone on the lookout for threats. And all of them screamed because the personnel who entered the docking bay were predators.

Your endocrine system was swamped. On instinct, you and a hundred others stepped back, practically forced to concede ground to calm your howling masks.

The figures you'd seen just minutes before now entered the bay: three figures, two masked. Only two—that gave you pause. Until you squinted and the central figure resolved more fully.

It was an android.

The android body was maskless. Naturally. Personalities and programming could be downloaded straight into their empty synapses. But without the visual language of masks to guide you, there was no telling what kind of programming it had, nor its prerogatives. You shivered as it walked past, expecting at any moment its blank face to turn to you. The other two were flaunting strength and power, both with their stocky builds and with their masks—a RATTLESNAKE and a HYENA. MARK IIIs, at least. Maybe IVs.

Something grabbed your hunters' attention at the same time RABBIT pinged you. The GUI in your mask fluttered to life, white circles spinning as they surrounded the tiny, half-concealed device in HYENA's hands. It was confirmed, then. They were tracking something.

You went cold and pressed yourself against the surrounding bodies. Your fear was not suspicious, though, not with RABBIT twitching, with prey instincts flooding your cortical implant. A dozen other people had the same reaction.

Had the appraiser not removed HAWK's tracker? Was there something in HAWK's complicated system that allowed these agents to find it?

RABBIT's audio capabilities enhanced your own, but you couldn't pick out any order or clean word from HYENA or RATTLESNAKE amid the murmurs of the crowd. So you waited, half cursing yourself, half sure that any movement would single you out.

But ... if their tracker was any good, they'd have found you by now.

The realization came slowly on the back of relief. HYENA held up the tracker—you didn't know the name for this tech—and pointed it in various directions. Starboard. Port. They were trying to home in on you. And you had to get off this planet before they got to you.

All the ships sat to your left, where the back wall curved like a wilting flower. Any hope of getting out of here lay at that end, and even if this only bought you a few extra minutes, you needed the time to breathe away from HYENA and RATTLESNAKE.

Your left foot was the bravest part of you because it moved first.

All right, Wylla, you told yourself, *head down.* Hunch forward. Small, and slight, and not a threat. Practically a mantra, practically programming; your body reacted with curved shoulders and a slouch that arched your lower back in a way that was almost comforting. This was how so much of the universe saw you. This posture was how you'd presented yourself, because it was so often the only way.

Don't be threatening, and they won't make a note of it. Don't be violent, or the whole lot of you are violent. Don't be pretty enough to draw unwanted attention. Don't stand too straight, don't be too confident.

You slipped through the packed crowd this way and you made sure not to spare any backward glances. You let your peripheral vision and RABBIT look for danger, scanning travelers, merchants, workers, and every other cog moving the corporate machine.

The bellflower curve of the bay drooped toward its end. You watched your own reflection in the curved glass, ghostlike and shy, hazy against the dark void of space as it picked its way through the mass of bodies. RABBIT's ears twitched faintly, searching for danger. You watched yourself like the reflection was another person, because it anchored you, kept your breath steady, until you were poised at the other end of the waiting crowd.

At this end of the bay, there was only the whirring of automatic docking systems and androids working to unload cargo from transport ships. You let the ambient droning calm you as your eyes landed on your hunters' vessels.

For military-grade ships, they were curious. Firstly, they were held in place by quantum locks, expensive things that kept ships pinned in strong magnetic fields. You worried that you'd need clearance to leave—either from BTW-02, or from the persons hunting you.

This worry bloomed in you like something fetid, coaxing latent cortisol out in a deluge until your heart was in near spasm and cold sweat blossomed at your neck.

Then, an alert.

RABBIT had been scanning the vessels. And what RABBIT found was interesting.

You didn't leave the crowd as you read the report, but you were momentarily so overwhelmed you had to lean back against the stretch of glass framing the black abyss beyond. But as you read, all that worry pinched and pressed into something vicious.

These vessels were not registered to the Martial Syndicate.

These vessels were, proudly emblazoned in the data, registered to VisorForge.

VisorForge. HAWK's—my—creator. A huge company, with prominent sway in the Corporate Federation.

And they were after you.

You didn't have the money for a jump-drive ship. You didn't have the time for a cargo hauler. Stealing a ship from BTW-02 might have been easier, but suddenly you didn't want to do things easily.

You wanted to steal a ship from the bastards trying to hunt you.

6

Those ships were your escape.

They were more than thirty feet from you, but at your back, your pursuers stood less than half that distance. You broke from the crowd and the lack of cover felt, instantly, awful. RABBIT trilled something violent and you ignored it with every ounce of willpower.

You pressed close to crates and single-focused androids until you neared the ships. This new cover awarded you time to breathe, but with a rabbit's sense and your cortisol already spiked, you felt your knees buckling to avoid airborne predators that weren't there.

You blinked away the prey fear and looked out at your chance for sabotage and escape.

Two tiny, sleek-black ships perched insectile with their gangways lowered; vessels of possibility. Their sophistication enticed you as much as the promise of escape, but your heart dropped at the sight of their protector. The android stood inert and rigid, its body an off-white bone color, its faceless, smooth head unsettling in its stillness. Your head swung back around, eyes locked on HYENA and RATTLESNAKE as they picked through the crowd, and your fear of facing the android briefly overcame your resolve, until you remembered there was no other way out.

You stepped out from the crates and kept low, skirting close to the surrounding machinery. RABBIT beeped steadily as you slinked around the back of the vessels and approached one of the gangways. You could see the android's legs beneath the slanted gangway, and it hadn't moved. Good. You intended to haul yourself up with the hope you could scrabble inside the door's shadow before you were spotted. Then would come the problem of the quantum lock and the clearance—you thought you would have to hack it. Which you could do, probably: you were brilliant.

You would just need time.

You shifted your weight, testing the pulsing pain of your injured ankle. It hadn't healed yet, but it was only one jump. You moved your hands into position against the ramp.

The rumbling click of a weapon being aimed at your skull echoed in your left ear.

You'd let them come up behind you.

Stupid, you thought to yourself. *How fucking stupid.* RABBIT's warning shouldn't have been ignored.

You raised your hands and pushed to your full height, turning slowly to face the blaster. No planet lock, after all. RATTLESNAKE stared over it. His hand was so large it seemed to eat his blaster, which he used to herd you to the front of the ship where HYENA now waited beside the android. You shivered when the unnerving, blank face whirred toward you.

"Silly," RATTLESNAKE said, gruff and low.

A thousand eyes were on you. Some artificial perimeter had been set up, and people bunched together, at once eager to watch and desperate to be well out of the way.

"Her tech is ancient." HYENA had an acid-bite voice, full of precise snark. She flicked a white-blond braid off her shoulder. "MARK Is get you nowhere."

"Sure this is her?"

"Well, the tracker—"

The rest was drowned out by adrenaline, your heart pounding in your ears. The android hadn't moved, but it stayed staring at you, eyeless face trained on your body.

"I'll remove my mask," you whispered, and they grew quiet. You stepped away very carefully—they barked at you, a little warning, but since you were reaching up to unlatch RABBIT from your head, they let you move. HYENA was staring down at the tracker, then back up at you. Her weapon was still latched at her belt, but in RABBIT's final act, before you pulled it free, it estimated RATTLESNAKE would take no more than two seconds to aim and fire. RABBIT trilled a farewell and you hooked it onto your belt haphazardly. Just as slowly, you freed HAWK from the sack and lifted it up to show them. "Is this what you're after?"

RATTLESNAKE's hand shook, blaster momentarily misaimed before he refocused. "That is VisorForge technology. You don't know what you have. So hand it over, darling, we'll be out of your hair."

"Not darling," HYENA whispered, looking you up

and down. A shiver went through you. What did she *see*? You felt a shame you should never have had to feel scour your neck.

Kill her, I thought, howling silently at your side. They weren't going to let you go. And besides: she was fucking rude.

There was a synergy between us. There must have been. Because rage flooded your nervous system: muscles tensed, heat burning your blood, your heart pounding in no anxious flutter, but a determined, percussive beat.

Without RABBIT you were estimating; at ten paces out, the android would still be on you in seconds. You didn't know how many. You didn't know the range of RATTLESNAKE's blaster, or the android's programming, or how well HYENA could aim.

You didn't know anything except for yourself.

And you were angry.

You put HAWK to your face and rolled.

Blasters rang out.

You rolled once, twice, left arm crushing the mask against you until HAWK registered and unfolded, tiling across your face and head until it formed a solid helmet.

And I sang with purpose.

In a second, the world slowed for me. HYENA's back leg was pushing off the ground to run. RATTLESNAKE was firing his fourth shot. To your right, the android was a finger's length from you, and a quick scan told me there were weapons in its forearms charging, moments away from unlocking, aiming, firing.

I launched upward and sidestepped RATTLESNAKE's

incoming blaster charge, bringing your body closer to the android. So close, in fact, that I moved your hand to touch it.

There was a kind of shrieking, a noise I think I made only in my head, and I could feel myself splitting. I jumped. I don't know how. It happened with the contact—could only happen with the contact.

I was both in the android, and the HAWK.

As the android, I gripped your arm and swung you back, so your body was behind mine. The act startled your hunters; they floundered untidily. HYENA stumbled to a stop.

"Report," she said gruffly, muscular body winded. Then, when I—the android—did not reply, her head twitched in worry. "What are you doing?"

Killing you, I thought, and the panels in the android's forearm slid open. A tiny, shining gun locked into place; I fired a bullet-sized blue energy cell.

It burned a neat hole into HYENA's exposed neck.

HYENA slumped forward against me, but the weight of her strong body was nothing to the android. I nudged her and she collapsed. RATTLESNAKE stood behind her, heaving. Thin rills of blood covered his mask, dripping from the front fangs as if HYENA had been his kill. He fired once and an ugly, searing beam buried into the android's torso. Hot sparks sprang from the wired cavity, and I couldn't tell immediately if something vital had been hit. I felt . . . above the android. Like a puppeteer rather than the android itself. I could move its body like it was my own, but I didn't have access to its knowledge or its sensors. HAWK, the other me, the other part, scanned and saw the android's central processing unit was lower in the abdomen, its power source just below. RATTLESNAKE had fired like the body was human, and he was shaking now.

"Stop it," he said hysterically. "That's an order! AS. Did you hear me?"

AS. Attack System. I felt the order spin up in the android's brain. The programming *wanted* it to move. The body started to heat up and tremble, error codes piling up. My grip began to slip.

As HAWK, I yelled at you, "Give me *your* order!"

And Wylla, you said, "Protect me."

You had a sort of poetic timing, because four hundred meters away, at the other end of the docking bay, the doors slid open and a horde of planet security personnel ran out toward us. A few screams went up from the crowd and the thick wall of bodies tried to flatten themselves to the ground. There was no time to think. RATTLESNAKE recovered from his shock. He threw the blaster to the side and launched forward, his mask humming as the deadly jaw cranked open.

Over the android's shoulder, HAWK saw it all. The venom in the teeth filling up, the snap-maw readying to lock on, the lenses in the RATTLESNAKE's eyes zoning in on the target. I was too slow.

RATTLESNAKE dropped low and bit into the open gun panel on the android's arm. I sent the order to shoot and it went wide, skimming RATTLESNAKE's left cheek. He howled as the charge burned through the byronnicum and blistered the skin beneath, red, angry flesh sizzling. Screaming, the RATTLESNAKE clamped harder. Metal, fiber, and cord creaked as the android's arm was torn free, and it was all very impressive except the android had another arm. With another gun.

It whirred out of its socket and I sent the charge into RATTLESNAKE's skull.

But you'd briefly let go of the android, and I could feel it start to fight back. I was slipping away, and HAWK screamed at you to step forward and secure contact again. The touch mattered, but your flesh was a poor conductor, and now that AS had recovered, it was actively clawing at me, trying to eject me.

"Not much time left," I told you as HAWK, risking a split focus. You were so sweet that you put another hand on the android, thinking the extra contact might help. It did nothing but make me dizzy with your kindness; I wished I could feel you.

"Choose a ship," I said, and one-handedly stripped both masks from our hunters' bodies, thinking you might sell them, and also snagged HYENA's tracker just in case someone decided we were worth chasing.

Planet security had spread out with weapons drawn. I kept the android body in front of you as a shield and considered my options. You'd asked me to protect you—I wouldn't let them hurt you.

But security all came to a grinding halt. They were hesitating, probably because whoever was in charge was reconsidering whether VisorForge would reward a few more gallant deaths. I didn't wait for them to make up their mind. I kicked the unlocked blaster toward you and you knelt to pick it up, one hand steady on my— the android's—lower back. You aimed over the android's shoulder and rested your face against the android's neck, breath warming your lips as it rebounded off HAWK's interior. Both of me were close to you, touching you; we felt like one unit, unified, flesh and spirit and resolve. Maybe I was happy I was dead, or happy to be whatever I was, if it meant feeling this.

I raised my right arm, little gun pointing toward the general mass of security bodies. And I tried to speak, but I couldn't: this android had no voice box.

In your mind, as HAWK, I said, "Wylla," and you cut me off.

"You've seen what I can do," you shouted out to the throng of security. "You've seen me change the very programming of this android. Let me go."

Your voice was thick and full, an instrument made confident. HAWK enhanced your voice and it went booming through the bay—and it didn't matter to me that you were taking credit. You sounded powerful and brazen, and you wore authority with such ease and calm beauty that you seemed untouchable at that moment. I was in awe of you.

The moment stretched out and the tension was haptic. You held the android in front of you, at once a weapon and a shield, and I could feel its mind flailing at me as if I were a weight it just had to throw off. We didn't have much time, but I couldn't rush you. Or the planet's security. You held your ground, and your arm didn't shake once in the long minute it took for the order to go through.

A dozen weapons lowered simultaneously to the ground. And there was a huge rumble behind us.

"You can look," I told you. "I still have control."

So you swung your head and grinned. The quantum lock had been removed from the vessels. Once I saw that, I raised the android's gun to its own head and fired.

The android collapsed.

You screamed a little, but I was already embodying HAWK again fully and could stop the mask from echoing your cry out to our audience. I still didn't want them to know you weren't operating alone—and if HYENA or RATTLESNAKE had leaked that, I doubted we would have been allowed to leave.

Both vessels were freed, but you chose the last one because there was a false safety in being boxed in by the docking bay wall and the other ship at your side. I could have told you which controls did what, but you didn't need me. You could see where all their inputs went and could extrapolate how they would affect the ship, and you flew us steadily off BTW-02, now the graveyard of your very shitty vessel.

And as soon as you were clear of it you punched the jump drive.

7

The first jump was completed within seconds, and afterward, we were light-years from BTW-02, at the edge of Corporate Federation territory. The last time you had been this far out, you'd just left home. You'd sat at the border staring into Martial Syndicate space, imagining how much worse your life would be if you crossed that line. Convincing yourself to stay, to endure a government you already knew.

I saw this in your memory, and not in your mind's eye. You hadn't even thought about it: you were excited by how you'd comprehended this vessel's foreign controls.

"Shit," you whispered, breathless. "You're incredible. That was . . . incredible."

Euphoria flooded me and it felt like I was dancing. I didn't say anything, afraid to disrupt this joy you had for yourself, and the hope you had for me.

For us.

You put in several confusing coordinates for the ship,

ordering it to jump, use the thrusters for a few minutes in one direction, then jump again to a random segment or sector, use the thrusters, and so on. Battery be damned: you were trying to shake the pursuers you were certain were on your tail.

All this time you were wearing me.

With the ship fulfilling your orders, you gave RABBIT the job of scanning for threats, and me the honor of watching you work. Immediately you accessed the feed and wiped your registration to your abandoned ship. Personal IDs were linked to vessels and were meant to be a permanent history of every one you'd owned. Not permanent for you, though. You were smart, and RABBIT was your coconspirator. You tapped into the GIRS.

It was here you were reminded of the reality of our situation. Being tracked by VisorForge was a new development, and you were worried RATTLESNAKE or HYENA had scanned RABBIT and found your ID, and that VisorForge might dig and find your old records.

It was an old fear of yours. You felt surveilled, haunted by your past. Under this system, you weren't criminalized, but you were marked. Nothing you could change would be enough, because in the end, it never mattered to them. The cruelty was the point. And corporations lacked empathy: they would absolutely flood the whole territory with your old details if they thought it would flush you out of hiding. You needed your records to do anything in this system; how could you live if they made you live as *him* instead of Wylla?

You let those panicked thoughts fuel you and dug deeper into the GIRS. From what I understood, this was beyond dangerous. Corporate entities existed whose sole job was to track these systems, and being caught probing could alert all manner of people. Now it was my mind that conjured Subsidiaries. I thought of a power strong enough to take you from me.

The thought must have leaked into your mind, for you snorted. "Subsidiaries are too important for the likes of me." The escape from BTW-02 had inspired you, and your assuredness was contagious.

RABBIT pinged every few moments, diverting probes, ready to scream if something found you digging around. But nothing did. You carefully moved into your own record and unpicked your old vessel's registration from your name. You orphaned it, and then implanted a new, falsified identifier to take ownership of your old craft. Then you moved into this shuttlecraft's system—very carefully, in case VisorForge had left a trap—but you were easily able to scrub the ship's ID and implant your own.

Then you told RABBIT to run queries in the public newsfeed for three things. The first: your name, your picture, your ID—anything that suggested VisorForge knew your identity. The next: information about the massacre on Pholan's World. This was a query you had RABBIT looking for in scavenger circles, too. And finally: anything to do with VisorForge and plans for new, experimental tech.

You doubted that last one would yield anything, but you wanted to keep busy.

And after all that, you briefly thought about me.

Why was this Martial Syndicate ship registered to

VisorForge? If the appraiser had removed my tracker, how had they found you? How did it all connect, and what had you gotten yourself into?

But you couldn't hold these thoughts for long. The world became fuzzy and you entered some kind of trance, before panic hit you and you were crying. It was overdue. You hadn't processed Pholan's World. You hadn't expected to see me kill those people. And even if it was necessary, even if I was on your side, you were . . . scared. Of me.

This knowledge rocked me. You were trying to keep your thoughts to yourself, but you still had the courage to be wearing me, after all this. I promised myself I wouldn't speak and I wouldn't show you anything unless you spoke to me first. I would do what you told me to do. I would try very hard not to kill people, unless I absolutely had to.

"I'm sorry," you said. I didn't know why. You took me off to finish crying. When you were done, you dabbed your tears from my underside and put me back on and just . . . exhaled.

"Do you ever—" you began, and then cut yourself off. "*Did* you ever feel so . . . stupid? When you were alive?"

I said nothing. You continued. "I like to think that I'm smart. Sometimes. Or that I have something going for me. But if I think too long, about things I've done or how I act or how I . . . am . . . I just think: What were you thinking?"

I didn't know what you were talking about, and I was afraid to ask. You might have meant what just happened on BTW-02—you were still kicking yourself for letting those agents come up behind you. But it felt heavier than that; your words had the weight of history to them. Something wormed its way free from a blockade in your mind: a dark thought, one of death, one of who you used to be. *I feel so stupid for thinking I could be who I wanted to be.*

I heard that and wanted to scream.

I wanted to say: *Wylla, I think you're brilliant. You are the only scavenger who could have found me and chosen to save me over yourself. Why have you done it? Why have you risked so much for a revenant? Why are you hurting yourself with thoughts of perfection?*

No human could ever live up to the standard you held yourself to.

"I'm sorry," you said again, because you had grown used to apologizing for everything and anything.

I finally broke my vow of silence. "What? What are you talking about?"

"You are—incredible. And fascinating. If I had the time, or the money, I think I could do you justice. I could learn all about you, and I'd be *good* at learning about you. We could figure it out together. Then I'd know what to do. But now? There's no time. Because I don't know what I'm doing, Sable, and as much as I want to keep you safe, I'm scared. Maybe I should hand you off to someone else."

"But I don't want anyone else," I whispered. It was selfish. Here you were, telling me you were afraid of me, of this situation, and I was trying to cling to you. Don't go. Don't pass me on. I don't care about anything else;

you saved me. You. We would be good together—you just said it.

Beyond that, beyond me wanting you, I thought: *Let me in.* I felt your anger rattling around inside you, but it was buried by fear, exhaustion, and sadness. Grief.

And you deserved to let yourself feel rage instead of all of that.

"Ignore me," you murmured.

"Never," I said. "It's impossible. I called to you, and you found me. You. In all of space, it was you."

You thought, *And I'm sorry for it.*

I said, forcefully, "Didn't you hear me, Wylla? I don't want anyone else but you."

RABBIT found its marks, blaring out that horribly panicked prey-screech, and you scrambled up to it, heart racing from our conversation. You acted as if I hadn't said anything, but I could see my words processing in your mind. You kept rotating them, looking at them from different angles. You didn't believe me. You thought I was lying.

I wished very suddenly for a body. I wished I could hug you.

You lifted the anxious RABBIT from its port. It had returned three queries and many results: you scanned but I could scan quicker, and I highlighted everything of importance with a neat glowing box in the GUI.

The query on VisorForge had pulled several articles, a documentary, and a HoloProp on VisorForge experimental tech in the past half decade. This was the gentlest of the queries, and you skimmed past it because RABBIT's warning wasn't for this. Nor was it for the results on the massacre—one instance of it, a rumor floating around a few scavenger back channels: someone had hacked the PMS, the planetary monitoring system, old tech that scanned every ship that entered the atmosphere. You hadn't been thinking about the PMS when you landed, because Corporate Federation tracked everything anyway, and scavenging was a legitimate caste. The flight manifesto recording your old vessel didn't matter *technically,* since you'd scrubbed your ID connection already. But someone might know you well enough to recognize that vessel as yours. And that could cause problems.

The fact that no major news station had reported on Pholan's World was a good thing for you. Shitty in general, a shitty Corporate Federation cover-up dismissing the dozen deaths of nonviable workers. But good for you.

Except in the end, both the cover-up and all your caution did nothing to save you.

What RABBIT was screaming about was much worse than any possible connection someone could draw. Your ID had returned a result. A dozen results. The feed was full to bursting with your face, your name—both *Wylla* and the other one, the wrong one—and your identification code. You had gone to all the trouble to change your legally registered craft, and now that, too, was emblazoned across the news. Your photo was on an infoburst that had been sent to every major station, and that meant your scavenger caste had gotten ahold of it, too.

It just read:

Individual with ID number N-7210–86-F-28-S,

Wylla Sotain, is in possession of proprietary information from VisorForge Solutions. Individual is to be intercepted.

(N for non-corporate employee, 7210–86 as randomly generated code, F as your gender marker—you'd changed that yourself in the GIRS when they wouldn't issue you a new ID, and it meant the whole world started referencing you correctly—your age, and S indicating you are a scavenger).

Your fears had been right. VisorForge had put a bounty on your head.

You scrambled up and grabbed HYENA's tracking device. You hadn't thought to look, you'd been distracted; and sure enough, when you looked at what they were tracking, it wasn't HAWK at all.

It was you. Your ID and your name flashed in time with the searching ping.

Genetic code left on Pholan's World, or some trap in the GIRS, or betrayed by the appraiser; however they'd gotten ahold of you, it didn't matter. They knew you. And they would track you. Your tampering of your GIRS record, and your experiments with your own body, still hadn't propelled you beyond their reach. And this did anger you—just briefly, before you swallowed it—because, even after everything? Every change? Every wipe?

And beyond that, with a mark like me, like HAWK, every scavenger worth their salt would be after us now. They had torn your caste from you. Made you an orphan. Fury bloomed hot and aching in me: How were you still calm? You would be cannibalized by your own kind!

Gently, you put RABBIT down. I thought you might cry again—I could feel it distantly, that hot pinprick pain of frustration, of desperation—but you just bit your tongue and forced that growing despair back down.

"Oh dear," you said quietly.

I almost laughed. Was that it? Was that *it*? Wylla, you were a better person than me.

"Sable. I don't know what to do."

"They want me bad enough to kill you," I said. I wanted you to get up. I wanted you to rage and kick and scream, and use that body of yours, feel with it, *do something*. You kept sitting there so I said, "Wylla. Don't you want to know why?"

You thought for a moment. I felt the curiosity like a pull in your stomach, but you ignored your own wants and clarified, "Do *you* want to know?" Your voice came out quietly and then you shifted, hands coming up to brush HAWK's face, so gentle. "Because if we look into this . . . If we find out who you were before HAWK. Why you died . . ."

I could hardly believe how much you cared for a stranger, a lost mind in a bit of metal—you were too sweet for this world. "You're worried I'll break," I said. Not a question.

An apology started to form and you forced yourself not to say it. "I only meant, if it was me, I would go insane. If I found out why I died, I mean, why I lost my body, I think I'd be too angry to stay still."

I wanted to see you like that. Not anger out of pain, I didn't want you to feel pain, but I wanted you to fight back again, like when your bold voice echoed across the landing port. Corporate Federation crushed and crushed; happiness co-opted by corporations, individualism at once encouraged and stamped out. And you were one of many victims. I thought I must have been, too, to be so angry in that message. But you ate every dissatisfaction; you swallowed the awful truth of this place, because it was what you knew. You had never lived anywhere else. You weren't a citizen anywhere else. And besides, *everywhere else* might have been worse. Martial Syndicate would have killed you; either for your queerness, or by your own hand, when it all became too much.

After everything, you still had kindness. I didn't understand. I felt every hot emotion easily, and every soft, calm one held no spark for me. Happiness felt distant. But desire? Fury? They formed from the same kernel, and I felt them growing.

I think I'd be too angry to stay still.

I thought so too. I thought, perhaps in my subconscious, I knew everything that had happened to me already, that was why I wanted you to open yourself to that anger. I couldn't keep the rage to myself. And I wanted something to be done about it. I wanted to tear it all apart. Everyone who had ever wronged me, everyone who had ever wronged you.

I wanted revenge.

"You said you didn't know what to do," I whispered. "But what else can be done? They have a bounty on your head, and they will wipe me if we're caught. We can't go anywhere without them following us."

You exhaled. Would I corrupt you? Would you see what had happened to me and grow hot with the same anger? Would you regret the day you had picked me up for what I changed in you?

But I felt your resolve harden. You had tried to escape your past before; you had told them who you were, and they still refused to see.

You said, "I don't want to be prey."

We were hunted. But we didn't have to sit here and let them eat us. I wanted to know for myself, but you were choosing now to arm yourself with the knowledge of what I was. VisorForge was pursuing us for a reason. If you could learn that, and leverage it, perhaps you would have a future out of all this.

VisorForge had already impacted your life; with sway in the Corporate Federation, they had been one of the many companies to define what good workers were. They had forced you into scavenging. You had fought too hard and too long to become this version of yourself, and the thought that some company like VisorForge might tear it from you made you sick with fury.

Good.

"I refuse to just sit here. I won't go quiet," you said. Then, you nodded to yourself. "And I want to know what happened to you, Sable. I want to know badly."

Wylla. You were fearless.

8

The HoloProp that RABBIT had pulled from the feed dated back to five years ago, which for tech like this might as well have been millennia. Surprisingly, though, it had been archived only a month after it had been commissioned—an extremely short life for an advert style designed to run endlessly and inescapably. It crackled to life with a chime, and you projected it into the center of the vessel.

HoloProps were used in physical locations. Cities, ports, trader stalls—places where the most bodies would wander through. It wasn't something accessible in the feed, which has flat adverts. But with the right amount of money, you could turn those off in your mask. Not HoloProps. They were designed to bombard you, to force you to think about the product.

This one was selling nothing. This one was an advert for something else altogether.

A trial.

You dimmed the vessel lights. A tinny tune reverberated around us. Some AI-generated salesperson popped into existence. He looked like an amalgamate of every race, unrecognizable and statistically average—which wasn't done for representation, mind you, but to appeal to as many people as possible. Just another Corporate Federation workaround; they couldn't even hire a real person for this.

Though who was I to speak? Was I still a "real person"?

The salesperson gave an overly cheery chuckle prompted by nothing and began his programmed spiel. A dozen masks of every mark and type appeared around him as he spoke.

"They gave you the tech we know and love today— but are you ready for their next ground-breaking innovation? VisorForge Solutions invites you to participate in the trial for the MARK I LYREBIRD.*"*

The jingle took over and the HoloProp flashed with text—a channel on the feed to register details. You checked it immediately, and it was long ago archived.

"RABBIT, can you access it?" you voiced the command as you plugged the mask back into the ship. RABBIT chimed and tried to hack it, and I replayed the HoloProp over and over in my mind.

"Anything familiar?" you asked me.

"No," I admitted.

Something flared in you—embarrassment or regret. I didn't have time to understand the scope of it before you pulled me off and turned me over to look at me. Such a *human* thing to do. You wanted me to feel like a person in that moment, so you held me up at eye level to give my ghost the respect you'd have longed for in my position.

"LYREBIRD," you whispered. "Not HAWK."

Like a new name would unmake me or change me the way it changed you.

I wanted to say it didn't matter to me, whether I was HAWK, or LYREBIRD, or OWL—they were just names. But I didn't, because I could feel you. I could feel your touch, which I couldn't earlier. Your fingertips were hot against me. A blush spread across your cheeks—you were beautiful; if I had a heart it would jump—and I realized what I thought to be embarrassment or regret was neither. The feeling that had risen in you was dread.

"Lyrebirds," you said again. "You don't know them?"

I can run a search. Or RABBIT—

"Old Earth had them." You paused before you spoke again. You'd pulled your great gray eyes away from HAWK's viewports.

You know much about old Earth?

"A little," you murmured, flushing again. A memory came to you, one you had tried to crush on BTW-02. At one point in your life, you'd thought about joining the Edenic Order. About giving this body of yours that you disliked so greatly over to a different force altogether. Seeds and tiny propagations, rat-kings made of roots; you'd have let your body be changed entirely for a cause you only half believed in, because existing in your bodily vessel for *something* would have felt easier than choosing yourself for no other reason than wanting to live. You'd fantasized about horrible, impossible accidents, where the only way to save you was to alter your flesh in all the right ways. You'd fantasized about tech that could change you in a heartbeat; had fantasized about android bodies that were real enough they could feel like you. So long as the change happened because it *had* to, then maybe your family would understand. And the Edenic Order fantasy was no different. If you could save some of Old Earth's species, if you could *mean something*—

But the fantasy had died when you realized that, to your parents, this would be nothing more than another selfish rebellion. Corporate Federation employed them, paid them, fed them, housed them. You did not bite the hand that fed you.

You cleared your throat and dispelled the memory. "Lyrebirds are long dead, but they were interesting birds, because—"

An exhale fell out of you.

Wylla, I am already dead. Just tell me.

You found courage again and dragged your gaze back to me. "They were mimics."

The silence was so awful I almost wished to hear that jingle again; Corporate Federation clamor, incessant and annoying. But all I had was the stretch of tense quiet. Your blush grew to cover your entire face. I could feel your chest and the tight ball of regret that had taken root there.

The implication sat hot between us. I had the memories of a dead woman and no way to prove I was ever her. And of the memories I had only fragments. It was possible I could be nothing more than an AI thinking itself alive.

I could have feelings coded into me; I could really be
HAWK and not Sable-grafted-to-HAWK.

You looked at me, lips pressed together in a thin line.
I wanted to say so many things. I wanted to think them,
to aim a barrage of hurt at you, because I thought— I
thought you knew I was a *person.*

Would you sell me if it was true? If I was LYREBIRD,
a mimic of dead human Sable? Or had you talked to me
enough that even that wouldn't shake you?

"HAWK," you whispered, "Sable. I only meant—I
mean, it's a possibility, isn't it? Let's . . . find out more
about who Sable was. There were only so many appli-
cants. RABBIT, can you find out? The archived channel?"

RABBIT chimed and you started speaking, just nothingness, just white noise. You were embarrassed and
talking felt easier than silence. RABBIT used the ship's
GUI to pull up the list of names. Twenty-odd—and one
name corrupted, as if scrubbed from the channel entirely. It was the last name logged in the channel, months
after anyone else.

Months. Like a last-minute addition.

"RABBIT," you whispered, and the mask chimed in
acknowledgment.

Don't, I thought, but it was too late.

RABBIT unscrambled the name, and a terrible moment
passed where the jumble of symbols clarified into an ID
code. And then that resolved into a name.

S. A.

Sable A.

You ran another query. The GIRS had a hundred-odd

hits for *Sable A.*, which sucked greatly in that it would take a very long time to vet all those names, and neither of us were sure if we had any time at all. We knew that the ship we had commandeered belonged to a very angry VisorForge and with a bounty out, the entire scavenger network knew what you had stolen. Corporate Federation had exposed us horribly. Your face would be broadcast everywhere. Nowhere was safe, but at least this pocket of space, a beautiful black void, stretched out uninterrupted in every direction.

We would need to dock eventually. But not now.

RABBIT and I went through the numerous Sable A.s, and you started looking for widowers. Marriage was its own economy under Corporate Federation. Some rights were granted or removed depending on marriage status, specifically a marriage sanctioned by the state. (This was important. Plenty of people married for love, but only the right kind of people were rewarded for it.) Fertility was its own commodity, just behind working bodies; since infertile men, women, and others could not reproduce, their value took a hit.

No wonder my husband was angry with me. I couldn't give him a tax break.

The search took less time than we expected. You found the widower first. My husband—my ex-husband. I had not been scrubbed from his records; he had been married to a Sable Alzian for nine years. At death, my body had been twenty-six. He was forty-two.

Except Sable Alzian was marked dead a year ago, and the body on Pholan's World had died only last week.

Sable Alzian.

Sable Alzian.

I threw the name around my head a few times. I held it there, imagined it rolling off my tongue, or my husband's. Or yours. And I grew so frightened I felt my tears prick your eyes.

The name conjured no peace for me. It didn't feel right. But when you pulled up the image of him on the GIRS—the husband, the ex-husband, *my* ex-husband— horror jarred my senses. I must have made a noise, a HAWK screech similar to RABBIT's panic, because you picked me up and put me on, and you didn't think as you did this, Wylla, but you opened yourself for me. You let my overflowing emotions flood you and you *felt them with me.* You shared my burden even as the memories dredged themselves up.

I revisited my death. You didn't flinch. And when the foggy moment came when I heard the gunshot, when I tried to find the image of who had shot me, you let me imagine over and over that it was my husband who did it. Then, when that no longer felt satisfactory, my mind moved in a flurry, and I saw myself shivering naked on a metal table, and I knew instantly that I was not there of my own accord.

I did not sign up for those trials with joy. I either signed up with a gun to my head, or someone had done it for me.

We both knew without saying it that he must have worked for VisorForge. We thought that together, instinctively and in tune with each other. But I couldn't remember the specifics. I only knew, vaguely, that he'd had some importance. My mind acted like a database would to an incoming query, and pulled up a dozen suddenly clear memories.

Together we watched my seventeen-year-old self carrying a suitcase into a cramped one-bed suite on a station. I was alone in the memory, alone with my thoughts, and I was still wearing my wedding dress. It looked like it had been stitched together from table lace—it had: I remembered an old gravy stain hidden in one of the seams. My home world was so far from this station. And I was shaking in the memory, seventeen and puffy cheeked and *scared* because I knew what was coming. I knew he would touch me, and I didn't want it to be him. It should have been someone else. I conjured her: a girl on my home planet. A friendship I'd wanted to ruin.

Is that why they had married me off? Or was it traditional on that planet, in that community, to sell girls off to corporate men? To breed a new corporate generation?

I didn't know. But I felt that anger, the anger and the despair of that barely grown girl, the anger that seemed to sit in my genes with centuries' worth of rage: *I am more than this.*

Now, disembodied and sitting in HAWK, perhaps I was less.

The emotions were so strong that I couldn't tell if I longed to go back. Did I miss that girl and her life? Or was I just envious of the body—the body I never got to use how I wished?

Because even when I had one, it was not wholly mine. Like you, Wylla, but different. Mine was put to work. Mine was meant to conceive. Mine was to stay quiet and dote and not dream of murder. But I did dream of murder. Often. Several fantasies moved to the forefront of my mind. I saw myself reflected in a tiny square mirror in the cramped suite on that first station, naked on a bed, in the dim. He was next to me. I was curled up around myself. Tears stained my cheeks, but I was crying from fury.

I imagined rolling over and suffocating him with the pillow. I imagined running to that mirror and smashing it and cutting his throat with the glass shards. I stoked all these murderous fantasies for years, even as we moved from ship to ship. Why we moved so much, I couldn't figure out, and his role was encrypted in the GIRS. You were too focused on the pain I was feeling to worry about hacking it. So we just let my angry, tired mind surface a barrage of disconnected memories, let them feed off one another.

"You were always in pain," you whispered to me. "And you were alone on that ship. All of them were workers. Were there other wives?"

"I don't know," I whispered.

Your voice broke. "I can't—imagine."

Though you could, in a way. You had imagined for a long time how your body might be used against you.

And then your stomach grew oily with your own anger. Sticky and hot; your mind was racing, and my phantom heart swelled for you, because you were angry for me. No one had ever been angry on my behalf. No one had ever cared. What happened to me happened to plenty of girls from that planet. Probably to most women in Corporate Federation territory. You and I were mirrors, reflecting all the awful restrictions the world wanted to impose on us. You and I were the same: women who, when they could not control our bodies, they tried to keep cowed by the law.

"He signed you up for the trials," you said. "He wanted you to bear children. And when you couldn't—"

"I don't think I was the first," I whispered. "I think he had married before."

You launched forward in the seat and pulled up the GIRS, scanning through his records. We saw two others. One was deceased. Another record was scrubbed.

Both had been under thirty at the time the marriage ended.

I stared at the picture of my ex-husband. Space-pale, dark beard, hair curling under his ears. He looked old for his age, with wrinkles carved deep around his eyes and forehead. His nose was pockmarked and he was gaunt, weak limbs stretched by low gravity. My body had been stronger than his, but I had grown up on a world with natural gravity. Mean eyes. I could just tell he looked at everything and everyone with contempt. But I may have been projecting; he clearly needed glasses and was ignoring the problem. Fluids shift upward in microgravity, and prolonged exposure puts pressure on the eye sockets.

His name was Fyster Alzian.

Sable Alzian hadn't felt right because that had been his last name.

You had started to cry beneath the mask, but you didn't take me off—didn't want to lose the connection. I felt that thought scurry across your mind and I wanted . . . something. I wanted to hold your hand. Just your hand. I wanted to feel you squeeze it.

But the next best thing would be fusion. To curl up inside you, beneath your breast bone, to be inside you—and it wouldn't be violent, but intimate. The two of us. A union.

"I could try to transfer you," you whispered raggedly. "Into an android body, I mean. Then you would have your own body."

Except it wouldn't be, not really. I could be erased, knocked aside for new code to override me. And then there was the issue of the flesh. Conflicting feelings hit me. I was too human for something without flesh. I wouldn't be able to feel anything. The tactility, the cold on my skin, pain, heat, desire—none of it would transfer cleanly. Vaguely I had the knowledge that every human feeling in me—like desire of the body, even the rage I felt swirling viciously in my subconscious—could not be so cleanly separated from flesh. I felt desire like a phantom limb. I felt rage boiling blood that was long dried up. And I knew an android would be a poor facsimile. I didn't want a copy. I wanted the real thing.

I wanted the body left to rot on Pholan's World. And I'm sorry to say, but after that, my second option was you. What I had felt as one with you, Wylla, was glorious. But I didn't want to upset you: I said none of this. Somehow you felt it. The muscles in your neck tensed slightly, and I braced myself. But you just reached up and stroked me with kindness; a soft touch that said *I don't mind that you covet my body.* I thought you would be . . . hesitant. Resistant. Your body was yours. You had fought for it. I was a bodiless void of anger and desperation hoping to slither in and take root. I expected you to tell me where to shove it.

"I know," you whispered, thinking of your solution and the android body. "It wouldn't be the same." And then after a beat, "I feel guilty."

I exhaled. "What? Why?"

You shrugged, but you knew. Your eyes were misty, wet with new tears. "Because I almost don't deserve it. You know, I spent so long hating myself that it's become a difficult habit to shake. And you take your habits with you, even into happiness. Even when you start to feel settled. I like my body, mostly. I like what I've made it. But I don't . . . Make use of it. Not how you would."

You were talking about desire. You were talking about sex. Some memory must have surfaced; a fantasy, probably. I don't recall ever enjoying what Fyster Alzian had done to me.

But you must have seen something I hadn't, when that barrage of memories flooded us, because you thought of it now. The answer to our question—*Were other wives on the station?*—was yes.

One girl, older, but more shy, mousy hair, laugh gentle like rain, too demure, too kind for that station—I couldn't tell if I had liked her much. Except that she was like me, and that made us intrinsic allies. We had found each other in shadowy corners of the station. We had hid from our husbands. I had enjoyed it.

But it wasn't enough. I had wanted the sun, the full

public ordeal of being seen and known. Accepted for what I was. It simply wasn't possible.

I realized then that you didn't like people touching you. Maybe it was a separate thing from how you felt about yourself, or maybe it was symptomatic. You yourself weren't sure. It was all a jumbled and convoluted knot in your brain. But your skin crawled at the thought of sex, and you felt, of all things, guilty for it.

"I can't imagine having the desire and never being able to do anything about it. That's all I meant. I can't imag—" You cut yourself off but you were too slow with your thoughts. *I can't imagine being horny out of my mind and having no release,* and I laughed. You meant that twofold, of course, since you'd never had the desire, and then because you had such great empathy: you expected it must have been painful.

"If it makes you feel better, I am almost too angry to notice," I said, and you laughed before a twinge of upset clouded your mind.

You thought of the gunshot. The sound echoed in both our skulls. Warm blood pooled between my fingers. Some reactive, sickening feeling spasmed in my metaphorical gut as it reacted to the biting pain of the bullet. You made a noise like muffled screaming and jolted in the pilot's seat, gripping the chair with force. "I'm so sorry it happened to you."

So was I.

"I'm so sorry," you said. You had balled your hand in a fist at your side. "So fucking sorry. You barely got to live; you sound—I mean, you *are* wonderful!—and now you're stuck in there."

Your knuckles turned sickly white and you took me off quickly. You spun me around. A frown split across your brow and tears glistened on your beautiful cheeks. A storm raged in your eyes, glinting with something I recognized in my seventeen-year-old self lying on that bed and dreaming of murder.

You smiled at me, Wylla.

And I think I fell in love with you when you said, "So what are we going to do about it?"

9

Revenge. Obviously.

The proper kind, too. No soft bullshit. No "revenge" like a thorn in his side, quiet, insidious pricking at the seams of his life. Nothing Fyster Alzian could ignore.

I wanted complete ruination. Or better yet: murder.

You felt it, too. You were too good, Wylla, because you'd never really considered murder before. You'd let the fantasy flash across your mind, once or twice. But you hadn't sat with it. Marinated in it. Not like me.

We were open to each other now like a dam had been breached, and even if we were to patch that hole, parts of us had already run into each other. A part of you was in me, and I knew that I was in you.

You gasped in a great deep breath and said, "Let's do it. Fuck Fyster Alzian."

And if I hadn't imagined Fyster's importance in Visor-Forge, perhaps slow bodily torture would be enough for him to help us—you—take your life back.

You clarified, "He was important, right? High up in VisorForge?"

"I think so. I don't remember."

"It's okay," you whispered. You were nodding to yourself. "We'll make him help. Before you kill him, I mean. Maybe there's . . . source code. Something I can take from VisorForge, either as leverage to get them to leave us alone, or for the credits. 'Cause we'll need the credits."

You were saying all this in a rush. You were trying to think three steps ahead. Meanwhile, I already had Fyster's head in my hands. I was sitting in the viscera of my imagined revenge, gleefully jumping up and down, and you were trying to make sure we could live after the fact.

See? It could only ever be you.

You pulled up the GIRS again to search for Fyster Alzian's address, still avoiding all manner of traps and corporate entities that existed to track unauthorized changes. While you looked there, I took a peek at your record. It had a picture of you nearly a decade old, when you were a scrawny eighteen-year-old, dark hair cropped short and choppy, and your eyes angry. I was about to dig deeper when RABBIT trilled.

It had found my GIRS record.

"Sable?" you whispered.

"Do it," I said.

RABBIT pulled up the record. It was grayed out, because I was deceased. Sable Alzian, maiden name Veonya. Twenty-six. Though actually, I had been twenty-seven when I died. Over a year had passed since my official death, recorded at the nineteenth day of Quarter Two,

Corporate Year 337. Now, it was the fifth day of Quarter Three, Corporate Year 338. You'd only pulled HAWK off my cooling body a handful of days ago.

Where had I been all that time?

I could see I had been born in the Alpha sector, a little planet called ATL-05, Alpha Terran Labor. But it was such a small world, an isolated community; useless empty fields spreading out. I had memories of them when I was a child. However, when you pulled up a shot of the planet from orbit, the scan showed an almost over-flowing population per square mile of land. I doubted those pretty flower fields still existed.

There was a list of genetic relations your eyes glanced at, and I sent your heart rate into overdrive.

"No, no. Absolutely not. I can't—"

"Okay," you whispered, and moved the display so the names were hidden. "We don't have to look at them. Do you want to . . . ?"

"Go back to Fyster," I murmured. You pulled up the display and I settled down into the comforting heat of my anger. It felt so much more forgiving than fear. Whether Fyster had pulled that trigger or not, his decisions had killed me, and so I felt safe in this mycelium array of malice.

My greatest concern in that moment was that Fyster would see someone had tampered with it and know, somehow. But you were calm. I shouldn't have doubted your skill.

Instead, I began to consider the details of our revenge. I wanted to make sure he didn't know we were coming. I wanted to do something violent. If we showed up only to have that man *know* and not *whimper helplessly* as horrible pain wracked him, then what was the point?

Even if he could see someone had scoured his records, he wouldn't know it was me. He thought I was dead. That would be our great advantage: the two of us as one, murdering a murderer.

You had RABBIT attack the encryption because RABBIT was craftier than me. Its fear-based coding meant it always looked for quiet back doors. I seemed able to adjust HAWK's programming to my personal whims, and given I was prone to anger, I suspected my attempts at the hack would have the equivalent of shooting it to bits.

Which probably wouldn't go unnoticed.

You asked, "Are you all right?"

I laughed out of surprise. How long had it been since someone had asked me that and meant it? I wanted to tell you that I had a righteous anger: that settling on revenge like we had felt like salvation. But I was scared; you were too good to kill anyone. Association with me had marked you a fugitive.

Could you forgive me for that?

I must have been bleeding these thoughts into you because you told me, "I think he deserves it. I've known you a few days, and I can't imagine ever treating you the way he did. You were his wife and he squandered you."

And I swelled with a muddled emotion: pride, excitement, awe.

Then, all at once, our stolen vessel stopped moving.

"Shit," you whispered. You put me down gently. Without the tactility, the connection broke, and I would be left swimming in the void until you deigned to touch me again. But this time you hooked me up. I felt everything RABBIT had uncovered pour into me. The name *SABLE ALZIAN.* Every record registered under that name. Medical records, the fact of my infertility burned into the GIRS. Reports of remaining family assaulted the edges of my mind and I had to close every pop-up, trying in vain to ignore the onslaught of information about who I had been before death.

If I had a body, I would have thrown up.

"HAWK—Sable, sorry—can you run a diagnostic?"

You weren't looking at me. Your fingers moved nimbly, an adorable crease appeared at the bridge of your nose. I stopped paying attention to you because you were distracting and entered the feed. You had RABBIT running a diagnostic too. I felt the outline of its presence in the vessel's systems, the AI jittery with its programmed fear, desperately searching for whatever threat might harm you. I didn't acknowledge it, and it didn't acknowledge me, since it was too busy protecting you. But I wondered what would have happened if RABBIT's AI reached out to me. Would I be some kind of uncanny valley for it? Or would it recognize me as one of its own?

I stopped thinking like that and focused. Intrinsically, I knew what I was doing. As if I knew all the systems of this vessel, everything felt like a second skin. I queried and found, much quicker than RABBIT, what had happened.

A second after you had plugged me in, I sent my own squawking chime out. I'd never made that noise before—horrible!—and instead of viewing my report on screen, you touched me.

It's the jump drive, I said. *The battery.*

"Shit," you hissed. "It's dead?"

I think it's been shut down. A weak electromagnetic pulse.

You splayed your hands on the console, slipping your hand away from me to have a private moment of internalized swearing, and then you touched me again. "Thrusters are okay?"

Both RABBIT and I chimed affirmatively.

"Okay. Okay. Then, I guess . . ." You pulled up the star system map, trying to work out where we were. We'd jumped to the Gamma sector, right at its fringes. Briefly, you were stumped. What should you do? Returning home was death. Your face was in every Corporate Federation sector. Who knew if it had reached independent stations or planets, and what they would do if they caught you?

How valuable was a VisorForge MARK I outside of Corporate Federation jurisdiction?

RABBIT screamed in warning a moment before I registered the threat. Out of nowhere, three craft popped into existence on the NAVIDAR.

On your first shitty craft, the one you'd rescued me on, they would have shown green on the NAVIDAR; friendlies. But Martial Syndicate owned and VisorForge registered, this vessel blared a warning. All craft were marked red. Three hostiles. The text *SCAV* floated above each steadily approaching dot.

Scavengers, your once brethren, had found you.

"No," you whispered. "No, no, no."

You went immediately to the back of the vessel and

unscrewed a panel. Slots for additional batteries lay empty; a single battery powered the engine and jump drive, and the EMP had fried it. It couldn't be saved. Angrily, you cursed, and rushed back to the front. The ship's guns had been shut down but were trying to wake up. The thrusters, at least, were responding.

But without a jump drive, we couldn't go far.

Part of me panicked. We had tried to cover our tracks and we had failed. The appraiser had stripped the tracker from me, and you had surgically stitched a new ID to this vessel. The only way they could have found you is if they had their own GIRS hacker. If someone had gone in, and somehow noticed the sutures at the site of your tampering . . . Perhaps they could have found you there. But you were *meticulous*, Wylla.

Or perhaps . . .

Your records, I gasped.

You picked me up, eyes wide. "What did you do?"

I opened your record, I said. There was no point denying it. *I wanted to . . . see you.*

"*Sable!*" Your voice cracked. You had never sounded so exasperated.

I'm sorry.

As if to steady yourself, you inhaled deeply and held the breath. Only then did you say, "They're looking for me. If you weren't cautious, a good hacker could have found the location of your ping."

With speed, you put me down again and checked your theory. You'd been right—our vessel had been pinged; in answer, it had sent out the ship's ID code, which you had stitched to your own ID, and our location. It had been broadcasting it for minutes, very stealthily. Even RABBIT hadn't noticed.

You had a bounty on your head, Wylla, and now your fear had come true.

To be eaten by your own kind.

Scavengers were thorough, and I was too lucrative a mark to abandon. It made sense to me these three had jumped in; if there was even one chance to get ahold of HAWK, they'd take it.

But not if I could save you.

I scanned and reported on the GUI: one of the vessels had a GTW-02 registration; two others hailed from BSIP-01 (Beta, Station, IP). The IDs tied to our new hunters hid their names, but all had their scavenger caste emblazoned. They weren't hiding what they were.

I started squawking until you stopped bothering with the controls and came to me.

"What?"

Put me on, I said. *They're going to board.*

"But if they find you," you said, and nothing else.

They don't know what I can do. Do you understand, Wylla? Our ship guns are still dead, and they're useless once they board. The bounty is on your *head whether you use me or not. Scavengers will strip this vessel clean regardless. So put me on, and let me get you out of this.*

You hesitated. RABBIT screeched, alerting you to a hail. The two station crafts moved into position behind your vessel, flanking to block any escape. But they didn't stop there. One moved in close, and I knew I'd been right.

They were going to board us.

They will take you back with them. They will take you from me.

You splayed your hands on the control panel. "RABBIT, open channels."

No—

"ID number N-7210–86-F-28-S, Wylla Sotain. We are here to collect the bounty on your head. Come quietly, and no harm will come to you or anyone else on the vessel."

They were certain it was you. But you could have lied. Delayed them a fraction.

You didn't.

"Please," you said. "Don't do this." I couldn't tell if you were scared. I wished you were touching me; I heard the quaver in your voice, but you had your eyes closed. If you would only pick me up and put me on.

"Stay calm, Sotain. It'll all be over soon."

You told RABBIT to kill the connection and then you turned and kicked the portside wall. The vessel clanged sadly and you screamed, quite half-heartedly; just stood and lifted your arms up to your head, squeezing the sides of your face with your elbows. Screamed.

Pick me up, pick me up, pick me up. There were tears in your eyes. You saw RABBIT, saw me—and you chose me. You put me on, and I was hit instantly with your guilt, because you thought not wearing RABBIT would make it easier for them to steal it.

"Okay, okay," you kept saying, a mantra to yourself. You put RABBIT in the burlap sack and started feeling desperately along the ship's paneling, trying to find somewhere loose you could pry free.

You forgot you were wearing me. I flagged a weak spot in a panel and you flipped open an electric screwdriver, hastily wrenched it open, and put RABBIT inside. Then the hull creaked and shook. One of the other vessels had a boarding seal and it was locking on. The impact made you wobble. You jumped down, cursing as your slow-healing ankle pulsed with pain. You got out your blaster, but your hands were shaking. They would shoot you on sight if they saw you with that, so you tucked it into the back of your belt.

The airlock trilled. Boarding commenced.

"Sable, what do I do?" Your voice cracked and part of me broke. "Even if I can kill this one, the other two ships . . ."

The NAVIDAR beeped steadily. The other ships had trained their weapons on us. Even when our ship's guns turned green, we wouldn't be able to spool them up without the enemy noticing—and before we could worry about that, we had to deal with whoever was boarding us.

It had to be us. It had to be me.

"I'll figure it out," I said, though I didn't know what to do. I thought about what happened on BTW-02, about jumping to that android—but it had a mind meant for programming and reprogramming, and it had been relatively easy to find purchase there. A human mind was something else altogether. I didn't fully understand how I clung to HAWK, how I'd been grafted to it. How could I wrestle a living consciousness out of the way? How was I meant to save you?

The doors to the vessel slid open. You went rigid. You thought about moving out of the way, putting your hands up, making it clear you weren't a threat. But your body didn't move, as if it couldn't hear you. None of the commands went through. None of your limbs were responding.

The scavenger stepped through the airlock. For a moment, he was just a silhouette. I felt your heart rate quicken, and then an unwieldy number of feelings bludgeoned you. Guilt, and horror, and relief, and sadness.

Because you recognized him, Wylla.

You should have shot him when you had the chance. You should have blown his fucking brains out into the snow.

The shadows resolved. He laughed at you, as if happy his gamble had paid off.

"Hello, Wylla," Orkit said.

10

Something was still wrong with the leg you'd shot, something he hadn't gotten fixed. This was a victory for me; I cheered in your mind.

Stop it, you thought sadly. I recoiled back so violently I wanted to vomit. Your guilt, your despair; they clouded the space between us.

You couldn't stop looking at him.

I hated that.

Ropes of Orkit's hair sprouted from beneath the helmet of his MARK I CROW, a discontinued mask type well-loved by scavengers. It had been meant initially for legal traders and merchants, to help identify the worth of something on sight, to price things fairly. But appraisers and scavengers had flocked to it. Appraisers because they could tell when they were getting scammed, and scavengers because it meant they weren't hauling worthless scrap across sectors for nothing. It was old, but it would do the trick.

Except when he stepped in and saw you, and saw *me,* I can't imagine what that old GUI was showing him.

I heard a soft error code beep out of the CROW. Orkit paused and looked more closely at you. He cocked his head and laughed, hollow and surprised.

"Why the fuck didn't you sell that?" he asked.

Anyone would've known from your bounty that you were in possession of contraband. But to someone who had been on Pholan's World, to him especially, bleeding out in crawling distance of the greatest prize a scavenger could ever hope for . . .

He knew exactly what I was: impossible to ignore.

Why did you make me wear you? you thought sadly. Orkit looked nowhere else. Not at the panels, not for anything you might be transporting. At least RABBIT would be safe.

Wylla, let me take over.

You didn't. You just stood there. He approached you cautiously with his hands raised, and you let him get close to you.

Something like grief flared hotly in your heart. I saw a flash of a memory erupt behind your eyes. You were much younger, your hair a misshapen mop, Orkit lending you an arm to haul you up from the ground, a stinging graze down your arm.

"Nice find, kid," Orkit said, and your body swelled, blossoming with a slurry of pride and attraction. You longed for the praise a man like this could offer you. You longed for his acceptance; you had left manhood behind but still needed its validation.

Then you thought about Pholan's World. Orkit howling as you shot his knee out. You thought: *Why did I leave him?*

He threatened you, Wylla. He was happy to cave your skull in. And now he had a predator's gait to him, an expectation that you would roll over and let him peel HAWK from your face.

So why did you keep looking at him like that? Why were you so willing to forget?

Orkit snorted. "Thought you'd killed me, huh?"

"No. No, I didn't." Your words fell out of you; you tried to lace an apology into your panicked tone, something that might convince him you had deliberately let him live. That counted for something. "I didn't kill you. You could do the same, Orkit. You could just let me go?"

"Wylla," Orkit chuckled. "You're such a stupid bitch."

You flinched, full of anger. He leaned forward, just enough to skim his finger across HAWK's cheek.

Which was a mistake.

Rage—hot, and old, and cultivated in the depths of you—fulminated through you. And through me, too: I sent it over to him in a sharp jolt that made him yelp. He wrenched his finger back like it had been burned.

"What," he murmured.

He didn't know to any extent, then, what I really was. Or what we could be together.

You had a blaster at your back. You reached for it, yanked it out, aimed—but he struck forward with immense force before you could fire. Even without the OX's strength, Orkit was three times your size. Your fingers flexed open as pain pulsed up your wrist, and the blaster went flying.

"Stupid girl," he murmured.

And you laughed bitterly, glad he had at least called you "girl."

Wylla, you have to let me in.

"*I,*" you said aloud, then clamped your mouth shut. You hadn't meant to speak.

"You," Orkit said, "are going to slowly remove that VisorForge tech. You are going to get down on your knees. And you are going to come with us quietly. Otherwise, I'll shoot you through the skull and take your corpse with me. Understand?"

I had been scanning all this time. I saw he favored his left leg; your blaster shot had ruined some tendon, and scar tissue knotted around his right kneecap. He avoided facing you square on, which meant he wasn't underestimating you. He anticipated an attack.

"Hey!" Orkit snapped his fingers in front of your face. "Empty fucking head. Are you listening to me, Wylla? Take it off, now."

I'm scared, you thought. *I don't want to let him touch me.*

You had told yourself you wouldn't be prey anymore, but you didn't know how to be anything else. When I showed you the information on his injury, you ignored it. You were used to RABBIT. You were used to running.

I wasn't going to run.

"Hey," Orkit shouted. And his wide, calloused hand slapped down onto your shoulder. You felt phantom fingers close around your ankle and crush the flesh with OX-strength in the snow of Pholan's World. You tensed so suddenly and violently you bit your tongue. Stinging pain and blood pooled in your mouth, and you had tears in your eyes, and then such immense anger. Decades of it. It all bubbled up to the surface just as Orkit pushed down on you harder. You were angry you had been born the way you had. You were angry you'd had to fight so hard to get to where you were. You were angry men like Orkit would always think you fucking broken, and that corporations could undo it all, and that you'd laid down again and again to avoid the blows that still found you.

Your beautiful heart spasmed with rage, and suddenly I felt every part of your nervous system light up, until I was the one who couldn't breathe, I couldn't breathe, I was dying, I saw—

Rain.

A hazy memory took over. Orkit's touch felt awfully familiar. In the memory, my shoulder burned from a rough hand, a strong grip that had once been reassuring and grounding, but was edging ever closer to controlling. My husband. Sable Alzian's husband. The one who had changed my memories from flower fields to dreary station walls, fresh air to the recycled atmosphere. His thumb pressed so firmly into my shoulder. The other fingers gripped the flower-stem thinness of my arm. He could break it. I knew that—I knew that intimately because he'd done it before. I knew the righteous anger he had turned on me when he learned my body could not produce the children he had bought me for.

Because that's all that marriage was in the end. A contract. I had violated it.

So he had violated me.

But it wasn't my past that enraged me now. Orkit was

touching you. He had already hurt you once. I knew what men like that could do.

You were angry, too. Together we unlocked something deeper. There was no name for that emotion, no containing it; it ruptured every kind and sensible part of me. It blew through my convictions, destroyed the lingering remains of my morality. It turned to rubble every carefully constructed thing I had been taught when I was human.

When I was alive.

Before that fucker killed me.

I knew, then, that I had nothing else. Nothing left. Everything good in me was burning away, and you could feel it, too, Wylla, I know you could, because you were screaming. I didn't mean to hurt you. I still don't know if I was showing you something, or you were feeling by proxy what my body had felt, or if your guttural scream reflected the feeling devastating me.

All I had left was rage.

Let me, I begged you. *Let me take control.*

You thought: *I don't want to die.*

And Wylla, I wasn't going to let that happen.

You slipped away. Was it choice? Had I forced you out? I didn't know, but you were gone—unconscious.

However HAWK's tech worked, whatever VisorForge was testing, I think I was the breakthrough. Because when you left the forefront of your mind, your body was an empty vessel to me, Wylla. I stepped inside. I took control. Your body became mine, your limbs mine, the flutter of your heart and your panting breaths—mine.

And I howled with fury I could finally *feel.* My

borrowed anger burned in your blood. Red hot and scorching, I turned it on the one person here who deserved to feel it.

Orkit wanted to hurt you. I would hurt him first.

He had his blaster raised, an arm's length away. He'd been watching me, screaming and thrashing. When I made eye contact, his CROW eyes widened fractionally. HAWK caught all the minute spasms; the shiver of his hand, the turn of his left foot as he thought about retreating. All this time he could have shot you. Me. He didn't.

If I were a good woman with a kind heart—

Well, what would that woman do? Would she let him shoot her? Would she apologize for the inconvenience of her tantrum and hand over HAWK?

Fuck that woman. I wasn't her, she wasn't me, and never again would I give myself over to a man who desired to sell me.

All this happened in a second. My decision, his realization, everything HAWK was tracking and feeding back to me.

Now, I reached out and swatted the gun away with my forearm. The shot went off late, piercing somewhere in the bulkhead. An angry hiss sounded from whatever had been punctured, and I spun into the half moment of his distraction. My back landed against his chest. First, I got the blaster away from him. I didn't wrestle it free, because you were small, but I brought your fist down hard on his wrist and his fingers cracked open in desperate staccato spasms, freeing the blaster; it clattered somewhere on the floor. I made sure not to look. HAWK stayed focused, and when he glanced down—just a second, if that, spent locating the blaster—I moved.

My shoulder grazed his chest. I turned into him, got so close he'd be forced to step back to grapple you. Then I rammed my—your—elbow down onto his right knee, the weak one. HAWK had lit it up with red, a glowing beacon for me to strike. I knew I'd hit the mark when he howled brokenly and crumpled. I scuttled back out of range as he collapsed. But he didn't allow himself to pause and hastily stood up.

You were thin, taller than I had been, but your speed felt familiar after the heavy android. HAWK maneuvered you again and again, identifying every weak part of Orkit, and sidestepping you out of the way when he retaliated. I barely had to think. Like the steps of a dance, I moved the two of us away from harm, and when an opening presented itself, I took it.

I wrenched the CROW from his head and looked upon his pathetic face.

I threw the CROW behind me. Orkit jumped back from me, flailing. He raised his fists high to protect his face, already an angry, inflamed purple from his exertion. HAWK saw at once every discolored scar that indicated close combat. Bar fights. Scavenging gone wrong. He'd never had to deal with something like HAWK before.

And hell hath no fury like a woman scorned.

His face was completely exposed. I stepped forward, bottom of your palm raised as my weapon, and I rammed his nose upward.

Orkit didn't expect the force. Not from your body.

Blood gushed in rivulets over his cheeks. He screamed, this animalistic, half-choked cry, and staggered around. For good measure, I slammed into his knee again, and this felled him. He landed badly and rolled onto his back, hands flying over to cover his gushing nose.

I took a moment just to stare down at him. HAWK was chiming, showing me all the exposed parts of his body, every way I might destroy this threat. I saw the blood pouring from his nose and the way his brows had buckled. Delight sparked through me. Delight, and a slow-growing awareness that everything about this thrilled me.

I think I could have killed him like that, bluntly, if I made you hit him over and over. But I thought about the blood and the way it would stain. I thought about you looking down at your beautiful marred hands and knowing what I had used your body for. You would never forgive me. You would never forgive yourself.

You, who had never known peace with your flesh, who trusted me—I had taken something precious from you. I had stepped into your body as if to remind you it still wasn't really yours.

And I wasn't done. I had to kill him. I *had* to.

You came back very suddenly, an itch at the back of my mind. The heartbeat we shared flickered, rising, and your hand twitched outside of my command.

Wylla, let me do this.

In answer, you twitched another finger. I'm sorry, I am—if he didn't kill us, his scavenger friends would. I couldn't let you die. The image of your body, bleeding out, alone in space, mirrored my own death too perfectly. You would not become another me.

I found the blaster. I pointed it at my mark.

Orkit's eyes widened. He took his hands away from his face. Blood smeared across his cheeks and lips, broken through only by tears.

"No," he said, with a whimper. "No, wait, please. Wylla."

No question this time. No taunt. *Wylla, please. Like you have the fucking guts.*

"You attacked us," I reminded him. "And my empathy is as dead as the rest of me."

Without ceremony, I shot him in the head.

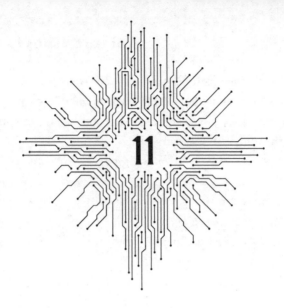

11

You were crying when I next had the privilege of your touch. I was . . . halfway across the ship, because you'd torn me off the instant you had control of your body again. You'd crawled over to inspect me. Your gentle fingers grazed across the sides. Bloodstained. And you were shaking.

"How could you? How could . . ." You cut yourself off with a hiccup just as the vessel chimed. Another hailing from the two flanking scavengers. They wanted their fearless leader to respond, but his brains had been pulsed out the back of his head and smeared over the ship's floor. I think some of them were on your shoe.

"You've killed us," you whispered. You broke contact to put a hand over your mouth and muffle a scream and only touched me again after a minute. "You've killed us, and you've used my body. Sable, I—"

With as much desperation as I could muster in my thoughts, I begged you. *Please, Wylla. I'm sorry.*

"No, you'll never understand. This is *my body*. Mine.

I made it mine. And you stepped in, and you— Your memories. What happened to you. I felt them. I felt them leak out, and I—I can't handle that, okay? I already have enough, and I can't add more."

Rage was overcoming me, and I wanted to drag you down with me. Not to suffer, but to feel it. To really feel it—you were running. You'd been running your whole life, navigating their systems and their expectations and their requirements, trying to live authentically without suffering for it, and what did you get?

Wylla, this whole world was trying to erase you, and I couldn't understand how you ignored it.

Is your anger because you feel violated? Or is it deeper than that? I asked.

You froze and then lifted me high, brows furrowed. You said nothing. But you put me back on, and it felt like we were staring at each other, face to face, poised on some precipice.

And I wanted you to jump off.

"We don't have much time," I said. "I saved us—don't say anything. I wasn't thinking about you when I did it, and no, it wasn't altruistic. It felt right, to have a body again. And that was shitty of me, but you would have dumped me long ago if you didn't feel . . . something yourself. When you put me on."

Powerful, you thought, then squashed the thought, as if you didn't want me to hear. But I already knew. You were just like me.

I knew it wasn't the murder that really hurt you. It wasn't the death. It was the use of your body without consent. So I gave the inverse now: my consent.

"Use me," I said. "Feel as powerful as you want. Use me. I'm sorry."

"I don't want to *use* you," you said. "I want—"

The ship beeped. It wasn't the jarring screech of RABBIT's warning—I reminded you to retrieve the poor thing—but a hail, this one marked as urgent. Your fingers quivered over the control panels, but you accepted the hail with speed.

The intercom fizzled, static from the dead of space crackling to life.

"*. . . Orkit, come in. All good over there, buddy? Shouldn't be taking . . .*" This was all said in a language neither HAWK nor I recognized. But you did. It was scavenger argot.

You breathed heavily. "I have to respond. Maybe a . . . voice modulator. I can cook something up, but I'd need time, and—"

With instinctual confidence I said, "Patch me in."

You balked. "To do what?"

I didn't explain; I opened up my mind to you and let you feel what I felt, to understand innately what I intended to do. I felt your heart rate lessen as comprehension nestled somewhere behind your breastbone, and you breathed deeply to ask, "You can do that?" Your voice quivered, not from fear but from wonderment.

"If you were right before, then yes. If I'm LYREBIRD." Experimental tech, with a new and dangerous ability.

You swallowed hard. "There are boundaries you can't cross. If I do this, you must let me give only what I want to give. I need to be conscious. You can't take control. This has to be us, together."

"Yes," I said, feeling shame curl in my network. I'd been wrong to step into you. It wouldn't happen again. It would be us, together. "I don't want to do anything without your consent. It will be Sable and Wylla as one."

We looked at each other, almost, in the liminal subspace of our joined existence. I thought about what happened on BTW-02 to the android. Then what I had done to you.

But this would be different.

Consciously, the two of us stepped back from the forefront of our minds until body and HAWK were half-empty vessels. I reached for you and you reached for me. We reached without feeling; you with your own flesh and me with the staggering nothingness that was HAWK without your touch. We became relaxed. Distant. I can only describe what we were doing as operating on auto-pilot: I gave no commands and you took no orders. Both HAWK and the body moved as one.

And you and I became we.

We leaned down to the comm, a fusion in thought and action and intention, and in the stolen voice of the dead man at our feet, "This is Orkit. Tech and mark acquired. Returning now."

We pulled back tensely but we needn't have been nervous. Barely a second passed before the static flared again, and the voice on the other line said, relieved, *"Good man, Ork. Had us worried."*

We briefly panicked—what did we know about Orkit? How would he reply?—but instinct told us to say, "Not getting soft on me, are you?"

A dry *"Ha ha. Come on, hurry up. And tell us about the haul."*

"Yeah, yeah," we said, and clicked off the comm. Then, I could feel myself distinct from you, like a dividing line dotting into existence between the two of us, delineating where you began and I ended, and vice versa. And I knew you were the same, squirming in abrupt discomfort as you remembered this was *your* body, and not a shared thing.

"I can't keep it up," you murmured, and our connection severed. "Sorry, shit, I'm so sorry."

"No, don't be," I said. We'd done what we had to, and we had no time at all to sit here in awe at what we had experienced. I watched you fight with yourself. You briefly leaned against the ship's control panel, sucking in breaths. I wondered how this was playing out in your flesh; when I reached out to check, I was assaulted by your heart rate, nausea, that unique, discomforting feeling of being alien in your own skin, the dysphoria of misalignment. I waited stonily, worried that rushing you would only make things worse.

Roughly, you pulled yourself from the edge. You collected RABBIT, which was practically the sum of your worldly possessions now. RABBIT had access to your credits, your identity, your everything—nothing else remained for you to take. Save for Orkit's gun—I made you take that too.

You boarded the other ship, moving sluggishly as you climbed through the connecting hatch. Dread made you slow.

The vessel amounted to little more than a cockpit and controls with a device for human waste at the seat. Seeing that made you grimace, but you took the seat anyway.

The whole thing smelled like Orkit. Your body didn't know what to make of that; part of you calmed, another part panicked. Both had you feeling nauseous.

And me, too. Fuck that guy! His brains were still on your shoe! He wanted to kill you and stuff your corpse in this tiny cockpit—Wylla, sometimes your compassion made you crueler to yourself than your enemies.

He deserved to die, and I was glad I'd done it.

"... *Ork, what the fuck is taking so long?*" one of the other ships asked. "*Let's get outta here. Plenty other scavs were tracking those records. They'll have pinged the location by now.*"

You hastily sent back an affirmative, which you hoped would be taken at face value, and settled into the seat. We had less than a minute, I estimated, before someone started sniffing.

If they hailed us on screen, it would be over. They'd see you and know what we had done, and open fire without asking a single question. This fear kept clawing at the edges of your mind—and mine—but you ignored it, not letting it get a purchase.

Quickly, you uncoupled the docking bridge from your other stolen vessel and used the ship's thrusters to align us with the other scav ships.

"Jump drive?" I asked.

Your fingers grazed over the relevant buttons on the control. "Yes. Full power by the look of it. But . . ."

The jump drive was switched off. This momentarily shocked you; every scavenger you knew, yourself included, had the jump drive spooled up and ready at any given time. Sure, it meant you were always burning battery at a low level, but it also meant you could jump quickly and efficiently if you were ever in trouble. Which you were. A lot.

Turning it on would draw attention. But what other choice did we have? You flicked it on, and the spooling whir began.

They hailed us immediately.

"*Idiot, the VisorForge station is in this same sector. We don't need to jump yet.*"

You waited. A knot formed in your stomach as you watched it spool up. Ten percent. Fifteen. Your fingers dug into the itchy fabric of the pilot's seat.

"Could you . . . ?" you said, and LYREBIRD chirred in acceptance. I felt my system load up—I could inherently understand the placement of files and software—and I found a dozen or so voices mined from conversations LYREBIRD had been present for and had stored. In the miniscule moment I couldn't tell *why* it had stored what it had; what the trigger was, why there weren't a hundred voices it had mined. I saw it had yours, Orkit's, the appraiser's. Then there were others I hadn't been aware of, names I didn't know but made me ill to read. I ignored them and loaded up Orkit's voice again. You opened the channel to the other ships and said, voice modulated through LYREBIRD's speakers, "Uh, just got a . . . bad feeling. Can't hurt to be prepared."

A disbelieving chuckle rasped in response. "*What the fuck are you talking about?*"

You didn't know. You were talking out of your entire ass. But the jump drive was at 52 percent now. If you could just . . . keep convincing them—then we'd be okay.

"I don't need this right now," you grumbled, in the argot. "Bitch had some crazy tech, and she fought for it."

"Shit, Ork, is she dead?"

And the other ship, *"What does it matter? Bounty said jack shit about her being alive. Her own fault she tried to fight him. What was she expecting?"*

I briefly wished I hadn't shot Orkit in the head. I wished I had leaned into my rage and used your fists to cave his head in. I tried to keep that thought from the forefront you could access, but something must have slipped through because you tensed, and exhaled shakily into the comm.

"And you said I was getting soft," one of them scoffed. *"Next thing I know you'll be an Edenic sympathizer."*

"Hilarious," you said, as laughter rippled over the feed, crackly and disjointed.

Eighty percent. Eighty-two.

One of the scavs said, *"Okay, seriously though. What is it? What's VF so worked up about?"*

"He hasn't told us. Bastard's gonna claim the bounty for himself."

"Shit, and leave us? Is that the plan, dickwad?"

They were laughing, but I heard an undercurrent of sincerity in their humor. They were worried. I got the sense the three of them out here wasn't a deep-rooted tangle of friendship. This was business. Orkit had brought backup, thinking that would be enough to stop us. Hah. We should have danced in his brains.

"Come on. I just got back. Need to pee." As you spoke, in the back of your mind, you summoned an alternate world, where you had never become Wylla. Your blood curdled. You imagined the man who you might have been forced to become. You imagined all the rage and anger and hatred that would be spinning eternally in your insides with nowhere to go. And everything happening now, the deep gruffness of the voice coming out of LYREBIRD that might have been yours, made you ill. This could have been you. This could have been you if you hadn't tried to love yourself.

A laugh. *"Ork keeping secrets."*

"It's new tech. It's got to be. You really thinking of running, Ork?"

And before I had a chance to yell about the dangers, you said, "Ever heard of a LYREBIRD?"

The line crackled with dead silence. The only sound for a moment was the whirring of the jump driving spooling up, and then the affirmative click that it was finished.

We were free. We'd done it.

But you didn't jump.

"Wylla," I said. "What are you doing?"

You ignored me and stayed bent over the comm, waiting quietly for our would-be murderers to reply. One of them gained the courage.

"Well, yeah. Years ago. VF abandoned the tech."

You asked, "Why?"

"'Cause it killed people, dumbass," the other ship said, laughing. A beat later and their voice had changed completely, turning dry and quiet. *"It happened on some moon at the edge of Gamma. You don't remember? Everyone in those trials died."*

Your breath hitched. At once we both recalled the list of names we had pulled from that HoloProp. *S. A.*

tacked on the end, the last entry, corrupted, but entered months after everyone else.

I was the last test bunny. They killed twenty-odd people and still had the gall to search for one more.

And something darker in me, deeper than the white-hot fury, the incurable anger at my demise, my death, my now eternal lack of a body to call my own, had its own thought. Which was: *Well, they were right to try again. Because whatever they were doing must have worked. I am living proof.*

Only Sable, you idiot, you are dead.

Of course, there was no telling if what I was—consciousness in a mask—was the goal or a complication. But if LYREBIRD's trials killed the others, either through the tech itself or through some debilitating after-effects, then I was still an outlier. I died on a random moon from a gunshot, not a fried brain.

Why?

When I came back to the moment, you had clearly waited too long. One of the ships understood. A voice spoke a random code, a string of numbers and letters, and waited. A cryptographic system the dead man you were playing as would have known.

We couldn't fake it.

"Turn off the comm," I whispered. You flicked it off.

And when their weapons systems began to spool up, we acted. You plugged in a random course and hit the jump drive, and we vanished immediately.

12

A stretch of time passed when you did not touch me. I learned later you were scrubbing the GIRS once more with RABBIT's help. You thought about tying your name to this ship, but you knew you'd have to dump it eventually. So you made yourself a ghost for a while. A small risk, to have your ID floating unconnected from anything. The next port we reached, you might end up regretting this; finding transport without a single record of past ownership would be impossible.

The other thing you did was have RABBIT send out a small EMP of your own to kill any tracking device that might have been sequestered on the ship.

You felt certain Orkit wasn't as smart as you; he wouldn't have bothered to trap his ship. His ego wouldn't have allowed him to think about the possibility of losing. The likelihood of a tracking device here was miniscule, and Orkit luckily had no ties to VisorForge beyond accepting their call. But you wanted to be thorough.

Then you set RABBIT on its final task: to finish pulling Fyster Alzian's address from the GIRS and disarm any of VisorForge's pings along the way.

As you did all this, you kept sidestepping something in your thoughts, like you knew the instant you picked me up I would look. Which was fair enough; I did look.

Were you going to a port, Wylla? Or were you thinking of dumping me out of an airlock? I couldn't be sure.

The next time you picked me up, you were wearing RABBIT again. Which hurt, Wylla. You were drunk off fright and latent regret. What we had done scared you. Nothing could compare to it; the tech simply didn't exist. And without this grip, this lifeline of comparison, it felt almost blasphemous to you. This information rushed me when you touched me, along with flashes—brief images of the Edenic Order, the clergy embedded with seeds and propagations, their bodies at once home to their minds and a new force. I knew what you were thinking. This was our closest reference.

But I disagreed. Or rather, I didn't want to have that comparison. I didn't want you to think of me as some grand force of nature, the seeds of the ancient Earth, which was now near a century dead. The clergy carried a legacy for a world they had never known. It didn't matter anymore. Not really. But us? The moment we had . . . connected—fused—*that* meant something. That was the future, that was evolution unfurling in real time. I wished you wouldn't look away from it.

I thought, *The giving over of the body to plant life is very different to us.*

Your shoulders raised to your ears, not in a shrug but with tension. "I don't know. I've fought to make this body mine. Sharing it now seems . . . like a betrayal."

And I heard you and understood as best I could and still said, *But you never really believed in that cause. You would have made yourself a vessel, just to feel like something good could come from the body you hated. What we have is different.*

I wanted you to know how I felt. I wanted you to feel it too. But I braced myself for your rejection, steeled myself until I could be ready for you to put me down and never pick me up again.

I feel it. Don't you feel it, Wylla?

You thought for a moment but you said, "Yes," and then tears welled in your eyes. You glanced away. "Yes, I think that's the problem. The whole damn problem. I felt like something—someone—new. I felt . . . I wanted . . ."

You got more than you bargained for.

You chuckled ruefully and leaned back in the pilot's seat. "Maybe. Or maybe I got just what I needed."

I didn't ask what you meant, and you didn't think it, or say it. "I don't know what to do, because I don't think I can go back. And I'm not sure I want to. Do you understand?"

I did, but in part only because your mind was open to me. It felt familiar. I could compare it to the day I kissed the station wife. You compared it to the day you left your family. When you chose yourself.

In that moment, I wanted nothing more than to choose us. I wanted you to choose us. However that looked like for you.

You said, "I know what you did saved me."

A defense bubbled up in me. *I'm sorry that he used to be a friend. But I'm not sorry—*

"I know." You stroked LYREBIRD's cheek and sighed. "Promise me you won't use my body again unless I say so."

I'd have given you anything. I could only give you my word.

I promise.

"Okay," you murmured.

Abruptly, then, you put me down. The loss of connection stumped me—it felt nearly painful. But then you picked me up with resolve, and you weren't wearing RABBIT anymore. Your beautiful bare face peered over LYREBIRD.

"I know what you are. Your nature, I mean. And I know that by being with you, I am . . . I make myself complicit. I want you to know that I am accepting that. Owning it. That I'm doing this willingly. I want to kill the son of a bitch who killed you."

And you kissed me.

Your lips, slightly chapped, pressed against the chilled byronnicum. You kissed me, Wylla. If only I could faint.

I couldn't exactly feel it. And I didn't know, really, what it meant. Friendship, maybe. A quiet kiss for my confidence, or to calm me, or as an apology. A dozen meanings behind one kiss—I think I was panicking. I suddenly couldn't feel you, even though you were touching me, like something short-circuited and isolated me in cold byronnicum. I couldn't kiss you back, but I was thankful, given I had no idea what you were kissing me for. I imagined standing before you with my body. I imagined you kissing *her*, body-Sable, chastely, and I knew I would have done something embarrassing like press back against you with desire, or tug at your clothes, and you would step back and tell me: *That wasn't what I meant it for.*

If I thought for very long about being a literal mask, it all got very silly. But if I remembered my body, the way it would unfold under a woman's touch, the heat and the want, I could feel some innate part of me yearn.

I said nothing, however. Without tactile feedback, I can't imagine how it felt for you. If I had a body you might have sensed me relax. You might have understood my eagerness, electric in my touch. Instead, you were met with a void. I sent nothing to you. I couldn't show you how I felt.

I lost all sense of time beneath your lips.

You pulled away. "Sorry," you whispered. "Was that stupid?"

I didn't know what to say, still hung up on why you had kissed me in the first place. Which only meant you heard more unending silence. I felt your heart rate increase, a soupy swarm of curses flooding your frontal lobe—*shitshitshitshitshit*—like a chorus.

You put me down and covered your face, laughing lightly like you'd fallen into me and kissed me that way. Like it wasn't a deliberate act at all. Laughing away how silly and embarrassing it was. I couldn't even laugh with you until you touched me again, and then I thought with as much humorous intention as I could muster, *Hahahahaha.*

The universe was a cruel, unyielding bitch.

I expected RABBIT to chime any second since it always seemed to put an end to our conversations via screeching. But there was no easy save this time. RABBIT's search took another several minutes, which we endured in complete and agonizing silence. Really, a single minute stretches awfully when you're aware of it. My own little millennia passed. I entertained the thought of shutting down and killing myself for the sweet embrace of never having to tell you I quite enjoyed it when you kissed my byronnicum bird beak, and asking would you please do it again?

You held me in your lap with your fingers gently pressed to my side. Not a firm, possessive grip, but a delicate one, and I wished I knew if that meant you didn't want to hold me, or if you were just being sweet. I could feel your emotions only at a distance—you were holding back deliberately. You were trying to keep me from knowing.

You like me? I clarified.

You scoffed and sniffled—were you crying?—and raised me higher so our eyes met again. The fish-eye lens warped your face. Crimson burned across your nose and under your eyes, which were glistening with tears. But you smiled anyway and laughed. "I don't know what I was thinking. You have . . . too much to think about. You died, you learned that fairly recently, and you're not— I mean. You don't even know what it means yet. To not have a body. And you must think me very silly— because you're not—"

The thought you tried to suppress—*you're not*

human—slithered through anyway. I tried not to react. Other thoughts of yours crystallized, striking me with their clarity: you worried I thought you predatory, you worried I thought you ridiculous. But I was thinking of Pholan's World. My body. How nice it would have been to meet you when I still had one.

Put me on, I thought, and you did. And when you did, when our vision collided, and your heartbeat became ours, I thought to you: *This is the closest we will ever get.* And also: *This is closer than anyone can ever get.* Because in truth, we were one person when we were like this. A fusion. And if I could not kiss you, or hold you, or fuck you, I could still experience you.

We could still be together.

RABBIT dinged to alert us it had finished its search. Reluctantly, you put your fingers on the ship's controls and pulled up RABBIT's report. It had found several Visor-Forge probes along the way.

Fyster Alzian was being watched.

His address was smeared across the display. Wordlessly, we plugged in the coordinates. He was on a station—GSC-05, Gamma, Station, Commercial.

Affirmed in our decision to take Fyster down, we resolved into a united front; all of our parts, however violent or strange.

You stretched out your arms, and I felt the satisfying unraveling of a knot in your shoulder. Then you leaned forward into the console. You began digging up the station plans.

I wanted to be involved. "Will we be flagged when we dock?" I asked.

"Yes. And this is a ghost ship, too. I scrubbed the GIRS so it belongs to no one. Which will be suspicious."

I jolted. "Then what are we going to do?"

You thought for only a moment. LYREBIRD was a mimic. You looked into me like I was a computer. Years of training aided you, and you overcame the strangeness of an internal search quickly. You found all my functions. You unspooled me and could see parts of my code and what it could do.

"LYREBIRD can spoof more than voices," you said.

Brilliant. You were so brilliant.

"You think you can do it?" I asked.

"I think *we* can. You're in my head, same as I'm in yours."

We could spoof an ID. It would mean burning someone LYREBIRD had stored, but to me there was only one choice.

Orkit deserved to be a victim of identity fraud.

I felt you react to that. You still had space in your heart for him, which I hated. I didn't want to believe there could be good memories of a man like that. I didn't want your heart to have room for anyone else.

"Can I please use Orkit?" I asked, and when you didn't immediately reply, I said, "He's not using it anymore. And he" [deserves to have his identity used for crime] "was cruel."

You didn't answer right away. You opened the station plans. Twenty levels of markets, high-end shops, and residential areas spawned on the screen. Fyster was sequestered on the nineteenth floor in a spacious apartment with its own dock and ship.

"State of the art," you informed me, tapping his private dock. "Those need biological material to open, not just IDs. No way we're getting in there."

Which meant we'd have to land in the station itself and find our way up to the residential area.

"Fyster's being watched and this station is pretty high-end," you murmured. "Orkit's a nobody scavenger; if we want to get close to Fyster, we'll need someone that can get past these triggers."

I thought about the station, trying to uncover a memory, but nothing came to me. "Can you hack into the station from here?"

You pulled up the network and began to work, gracefully unlocking door after door until you were sitting outside the station's security system. "I can try. What are you thinking?"

"Who has access to Fyster Alzian's quarters?"

It didn't take you long. You found the system for Fyster's front door. It wasn't as high-end as his private dock—no biological material was needed to get in—but the list showed only a few names.

Fyster Alzian.

Station Security.

Sable Alzian.

We lapsed into silence at the sight of that name. It hadn't been deleted.

"I can spoof Sable Alzian," I murmured.

I felt your heart drop.

If VisorForge was watching Fyster like we expected, then the use of Sable Alzian's ID would most definitely alert them to our location.

Yet there was no other way for us to get to Fyster's physical location. Embracing the trap was a necessity.

What else could we do?

"Let them come," you said finally. "We get in, we make Fyster give us leverage, and then we kill him. After that, we're gone."

Your surety made you powerful. I reveled in this side of you.

"Let them come," I agreed, and a covenant was made.

We sat together for a while as this one being. Existing close to you, your warmth on me and in me, our shared heartbeat and organs and limbs, was divine. A holy thing. An evolution.

We were something new.

13

You waited until we landed to change my record from "dead" to "alive," and quickly stitched Sable to the stolen vessel you'd wiped.

"We need all the time we can get," you'd explained. "We might be able to fool the tech here, but this record change will alert VisorForge right away."

Your greatest feat was hacking Orkit's gun. You'd tinkered with it directly, using the vessel's electric screwdriver to open its panel before plugging it into the ship's computer.

"I've programmed it to transmit a false ID. Anyone who scans this now will see an electric screwdriver," you said with a wink. No planet lock would affect the gun now.

You put me on and got ready to leave, strapping RABBIT at your side. Three breaths in, three breaths out, and you opened the hatch.

We were greeted by an AI in an ancient-looking touchscreen that seemed to take its job very seriously.

It whirred closer and asked us a multitude of questions, first about whether we lived here, and then who we were visiting, and why. It made no mention of the gun hidden at your waist.

"Fyster Alzian," you said in your sweetest voice. And then, "I'm his wife."

The AI made a noise of incomprehension before informing us of the impossibility of our statement. Sable Alzian was dead.

"You're mistaken," I said through you. "We had a falling-out, and I haven't seen him in years. But as you can see, I am very much alive."

I let the AI pull up the GIRS. I hovered in the shadows of the system, waiting to trap and purge it if it began to ping a human-operated system. But it was easily satisfied. "Have a nice visit, Sable Alzian."

It whirred away and left us. You swelled with pride: you had been right about what LYREBIRD could accomplish. I wish I could have squeezed your hand.

We didn't linger. As we moved into the station proper, the unattractive aesthetic of the docks disappeared behind extensive paneling. The cleanliness of the place confronted you. GSC-05 stretched over twenty levels, a vaulting mess of high-end merchants and shops. Synthetic fabrics to handwoven clothing; artificial foods and the real deal—herbs, live plants, even expensive live cattle; a bustling ordeal of markets for the wealthy. Ads vied for your attention, clogging in LYREBIRD's periphery, promising to leave you alone for a meager payment. Luxury shops lined the upper levels. At the very top lay a hundred-odd residential apartments.

The AI's questions at the dock should have clued us in—merely existing here was a privilege reserved for the right sort of people. We had spent so long concerned with our official identity that neither of us had considered the reality of our appearance in a place like this. Out of habit, you dressed to hide, to be small. We were starkly drab where others were clamped into form-fitting, stiff clothing. We stuck to the sides and walked up stairwells, staying out of sight as much as we could. But I felt the weight of eyes on your shoulders, the learned disgust you were breathing in. Like a disease, their glares burrowed beneath your skin, and soon you were thinking: *I'm not supposed to be here.*

Looking back, I wonder if he would have stopped us if we'd walked with confidence. Whether with the right bravado we might have passed off your dirty scraps as avant-garde chic.

No matter. It happened.

"Halt!"

You went rigid.

Calm, I thought to you. *You are Sable Alzian. You belong here.*

You turned to him. He wore a MARK III DOG, its helmet-like shape covering any identifiable feature, anonymity further aided by the neck-high black uniform. He was rendered perfectly conventional.

"Ma'am, are you lost? You, uh . . ." You felt him assessing you. The DOG's sensors widened as he inhaled; he'd smell sweat, coolant. Maybe blood on your shoe from Orkit's brains.

Perhaps there was no point in staying calm. I thought, *Maybe we should kill him.*

You thought back to me: *Let me try another way, first.*

"I need to get home to my husband," you said.

He stared at you, unconvinced. "I need to pull up your record," he said.

You waited. You let him dig into the GIRS, hoping he didn't know about Sable Alzian that way the AI had.

He read every line of the ID with meticulous care.

"I've had . . . a very bad day. This is very embarrassing," you choked. You glanced around, hunkered lower when you saw people looking your way. "You must understand how mortifying it is to be looking like this. I need to—I need to get home."

He pulled out of the GIRS to answer. "Bad day, huh?" LYREBIRD registered DOG's movements. He was still scanning you. He didn't tense looking at LYREBIRD, though I wondered what his sensors were showing him. "Why don't you come with me and tell me about it? I can contact Mr. Alzian and—"

"No. You can't possibly interrupt him, not at work." I don't know who you were manifesting, then. Perhaps it was simply the air of being around such rigid, wealthy people: you adopted a confidence I'd never before seen on you. "I'd be happy to tell him you kept me, though. Left me exposed and humiliated in front of my peers. What was your name, Mr. . . . ? Your ID?"

You were drawing interest. People whispered—most definitely because you looked like a vagabond, but you were banking on security weighing his own position in his mind.

He flinched eventually and gently shook his head.

"I'm sure that won't be necessary, Mrs. Alzian. Please get yourself home and taken care of."

You hesitated; our shared heart raced and you were briefly overwhelmed that your ruse had been successful. You made a noise of overweening indignation and turned on your heel. Relief flooded our synapses; yes! Yes, we'd done it!

Then a station-wide alarm rang out.

You stilled, as did everyone around you. Chatter fell away to a straining silence, and an automated voice rebounded off the metal walls: "*Security breach on Station GSC-05. Beware fugitive Wylla Sotain, ID number N-7210–86-F-28-S. VisorForge personnel are approaching. Prepare for immediate docking. No ships, personal or cargo, are authorized to leave the station.*"

Your face sprang up in holographic casts. All older photos, none with you wearing me. But the report gave your height, weight, and anyone with a decent mask could track those stats.

VisorForge had been so damn quick. I'd thought we'd have more time.

Behind you, a blaster whirred as it spooled up.

My Wylla, you spun back around just as security drew his weapon on you. You had the speed he lacked, and all your fearful hesitation evaporated: I barely recognized you. Before he could take the shot, you fired.

Right through the head. A hole burned through the DOG and into his brainpan. He collapsed into a heap.

Screams echoed through the halls of GSC-05 and before we'd had a chance to breathe, the lights went out as the station locked down. All hovering adverts were snuffed out. Animals bayed and more terrified noises echoed around us as people fled. Emergency lighting sprang to life and lit everything in a bluish haze. When you looked down at the blood and brain matter leaking from the security's head, the light made it purple.

I shouted, "We have to move!"

You protected me the way I protected you from Orkit, and before shock or guilt could settle in your chest, I overrode the emotions. I let you feel righteous for the murder and together we ran.

Another announcement blared around us: "*Expect VisorForge personnel in fifteen minutes.*"

We said nothing to each other, but we felt that pressure bearing down on us.

Fyster lived on the fourth residential floor. We were absorbed into a crowd of residents rushing the stairs to return to their quarters. But by the fourth floor, we were alone.

These halls were eerily quiet, cramped black corridors that lit up with clinically fluorescent light when triggered by motion sensors. Every step sent another light clanking to life and shutting off behind us when we were out of range.

Sweat pricked on your lower back, your armpits; two people's anxiety seeping through your pores. You kept our breathing steady because I'd forgotten how to use lungs and kept accidentally hyperventilating. But I could tell your anxiety was reaching a peak and clawing for your attention.

"Ignore it," I begged you. "I have to do this."

"*We*," you amended, and if I had been a body next to you, I would've taken your hand and squeezed it.

When we reached Fyster's door, we froze. The door looked identical to all the others. Nothing that screamed: *This man killed me. This man is a murderer.* Knowing how seamlessly he could blend into the world made me uncomfortable. I wanted him to be ostracized. Known and hated.

I wanted him dead.

There was a bell to ring, and you reached for it on instinct.

"Don't ring it," I whispered.

Dust had gathered over the bell. An electronic sign on the door requested all deliveries to be placed with station reception; Fyster Alzian was not to be disturbed. He was inside. Even when I had been alive, even when I'd lived here for three years, the man had rarely left.

And we didn't need to alert him to our presence. We were Sable Alzian in that moment, and he hadn't bothered to delete our permissions from his door.

I let the door scan LYREBIRD.

We hovered tensely, waiting for an alarm, or for Fyster to wrench the door open, gun to our temple. Nausea made us so ill that I felt it edging out of our pores. But then a happy chime sounded, a *ding-a-ling* as if the door was happy to see me.

"Welcome home, Sable Alzian."

14

You turned and hacked the lock so it could only be opened from the inside. Then we took our blaster out of the holster and raised it.

The door had opened onto another dark vestibule. Soft, muted light glowed orange farther down, spilling out of a room. The sitting room. I knew that, distantly.

A dozen memories flailed for our attention. Layered ghosts crossed this threshold hundreds of times, the path my body had walked the years I'd lived here. We watched as past versions of Sable walked down the hall, pushed into rooms, turned left toward that glow.

We stood frozen at the door, but down the hall we heard the clink of a glass. A chair groaned, relieved of its weight. And my murderer said, "Hello?"

We both jolted. You pressed us against the wall for a bit of cover and we moved silently, blaster aimed at the shadows.

A figure rounded the corner. The silhouette was a haunting; I had seen him so many times. I knew the shape of him. I knew his size. Fyster Alzian was taller than you, elongated from low gravity, but strong. My memory said he had weight that could hold you down. Something must have happened, because this silhouette was thinner and much less of an imposing presence. He didn't look like a monster.

We walked forward and pressed the blaster to his forehead, crowding him back into the sitting room. He gasped—which sounded musical—and the soft lamp glow showed me he had grown gaunt. Time and disuse had eaten at his muscles. Exhaustion had hardened his face. His eyes were dead. There used to be a violence in them, a thrill at his size and his weight and his strength; he reveled in what he could do to a body, and he had been confident in how he moved through the world. Now I barely recognized him, as if he had been humbled so greatly it had affected his very flesh.

"Who are you?" His tone lacked fear, as if he'd been expecting such a thing for weeks. But I wanted him cowering. I wanted him on his knees begging for his life.

So we forced him down. "Go. On your knees."

He went slowly, groaning from an old injury to his hip. As he went, I surveyed the room—not much had changed. There was one big wingback chair, a carpet, a light. Plates of old food and half-empty glasses littered the floor, like he hadn't left this apartment in weeks. The entire far left wall was taken up by screens; locations of every VisorForge holding, a design for a new mask in the feline range.

He had been a liaison. I remembered that now. We had gone from station to station to sell new designs, to stock certain masks in certain stations; to force scavengers to frequent certain sectors for masks that would benefit them, to force foreign government bodies like the Martial Syndicate to travel deep into Corporate Federation territory for anything they wanted. He had been at the forefront, orchestrating and manipulating. Remote work could mean anything, but his demeanor suggested a demotion.

"I don't think I'm who you want," he whispered from the floor. Pathetic. I wanted him fighting. I wanted him suffering.

"You are exactly who I want, Fyster Alzian," we said.

He froze.

We had spoken with my—Sable's—voice.

His wide eyes tracked over the mask. Realization was slow, treacherously slow, as it unfolded across his face. I watched his eyebrows relax minutely as shock bludgeoned him. He dropped his arms.

"No," he gasped. His hands began to shake.

"Yes. Get up."

"Who are you? You, I mean. Where did you get that? She—she wasn't—*they were supposed to dismantle the damn thing.*"

We wrenched him up and he hissed as his hip gave way, staggering back to collapse in the wingback chair.

He flailed as he fell, shouting hurriedly, "VisorForge is already on their way. I heard the security message. They'll be here soon. Subsidiaries, even!"

Subsidiaries? He sounded desperate, and you already doubted they even existed. Together we decided it was a bluff.

"Put me on him," I told you.

"We have maybe ten minutes before the guards get here and find a way in. Find out what you can."

"I will."

Carefully, you removed me. A flower unblooming; the metal panels that curved around your skull like a helmet retracted, and our connection was lost. Fyster stared at you, eyes narrowing like he expected to recognize the face beneath the mask.

"Your wife wants to talk to you," you said, blaster still trained.

Fyster's face fell. "What?" His eyes dropped to LYRE-BIRD and a dawning horror bloomed. "No. She's dead."

"Not quite."

He jerked around but with the blaster aimed for him, what could he do? His eyes flicked between the blaster and LYREBIRD, and I warned you that he was thinking of lunging. So you pointed the blaster to his shin and fired.

Fyster howled. Singed flesh and linen burned hotly. The entire room stank of it suddenly, and Fyster was still screaming, bent forward over the wound. A soft beep registered in his quarters' system; an alert had been sent to station security. But we'd expected that. We had to be quick.

"Bitch. Bitch. Fucking *bitch*."

You were shaking, but only slightly. I think you hated him as much as I did. I think I'd bled into you, and you knew too much to be impartial. You'd experienced him firsthand.

"Stay put," we said, very calmly. No fear shook our

voice. And Fyster peeled himself off his wounded leg with a hiss, and rolled his shoulders back like a man waiting for an execution. He let you place LYREBIRD on his head.

It was ... horrible. Wylla, you felt like home. You were that field of white flowers on my home planet. You were the touch I had stolen from that wife on the station. You were every bit of happiness I had taken for myself throughout my life. And Fyster was the opposite. Touching his mind felt corrosive. He was violent, possessive, imposing. He made me feel shame for everything I loved about myself. A swamp-like consistency existed in his head, and by touching it I could feel myself growing sad and lost, an internal ugliness that wanted to corrupt me.

I did not want to fuse with him. I wanted that to be our thing. But his mind was so thick I could find no other way to learn what I wanted to know.

So I slipped into him. He didn't open the way you did. I had to claw for it. I imagined myself as Sable, the body, and I took my fingernails and raked them down his side, over and over again until he was scraped and bleeding. Fyster shouted, relenting enough to let me in.

"Hello," I said.

He balked, shocked to see me. I stood before him as the wife he had murdered, and I saw him as the man he had once been, strong and bulky.

"You're dead," he said flatly.

"You marked me dead a year ago," I said. "In the GIRS. But I only died a week ago, on Pholan's World."

His eyes flickered. Had he not known?

Fyster looked down at his hands and picked at

something, a ridiculous human tic given this construct wasn't real. He tried for careless ease but his body shook. "I didn't mark you dead," he said defensively. "The company did."

"They changed my record?" I asked. I stepped toward him—this was the information I longed for. Before I killed Fyster, I wanted to know everything that had led to my demise. "Why?"

He looked at me like I was insane, or stupid, or both. "Because she *didn't* die. Everyone else in those trials died except her. No one could figure out why. So they wanted to keep Sable. Run more tests, you know?"

He said it all so nonchalantly. I couldn't comprehend his calm. His apathy. It was the *lack* that got to me: the lack of care, the lack of concern, the lack of apology. Even now, even after he'd killed me, after he'd been so clearly demoted, he saw his wife and he acted like he was in control.

How could anyone be like this? How had Fyster Alzian gone through life without someone hurting him very, very intensely? It was all I could think about.

Rage boiled in me, and I thought about cooking his brain, about destroying him so completely he'd become soup. Enough pain could breach that damned apathy; I knew the searing torture of his insides burning would make him regret ever marrying me.

I spat, "You put me in there. You gave me to those trials knowing or hoping I would die, the instant you realized I couldn't bear you children. So you gave me to VisorForge, for their experiments. How could you do that? You took me from my planet, you did whatever you wanted to me, and then you *threw me away.*"

He sucked his teeth and looked at me with heavy disgust. "Stop it, would you?" He gestured at me. "Stop pretending to be my dead fucking wife and tell me what you want."

"I am your wife, and I want justice."

"That bitch is dead!"

We were both panting. I knew I was close to crying so I squared my shoulders and looked him in the eye. "By the time I'm done with you, you'll wish I was."

He backed away from me. "But she is. Sable is. You—you're some copy. You know that, right? You are not Sable Alzian. She died. You are just code that's mimicking her."

I shook my head. He was . . . trying to manipulate me. A stupid ploy.

"No," I said firmly. "No, I *am* her. I remember it all. I remember. And I know you killed me."

His expression changed. I thought I had him, but then his eyes softened, and he exhaled, slapped his thigh. "No, I didn't." I frowned. I didn't prompt him. He looked at me, grin splitting open his lips, and he said with almost sadistic glee, "You're a fucking artificial copy, and you can't even remember the most important thing that ever happened to that stupid girl from a backwater planet. Sable killed herself."

I—

What?

Then: I felt it. The gunshot wound rummaged into

my guts, piercing everything; hot, sticky blood dripping down my sides.

I looked down. A gun was aimed at my stomach. No wound had punctured through yet; time collided. The memory of the gunshot wound and the memory of the moments leading up to it occurred concurrently. Both of my hands gripped the gun, and I was shaking, staring out of LYREBIRD's eyes.

"Let me go," I'd said. I heard my voice—strange and high—crack as I spoke. The space around me resolved into a craft. We were traveling together. I'd left the trials or been taken; I couldn't work it out.

"You stupid bitch," Fyster murmured. He looked quietly enraged and nothing more. "You stole it. *Bitch*. Stupid girl. Now you've fucked us. Take it off."

I swallowed. "I can't."

Fyster stood and tried to rip it from my face. His expression dripped off him with sudden revulsion. "You fused it? That'll rot your face off. What the fuck is wrong with you? Now I have to remove it." He muttered, sat back down. I knew he thought I was insane.

I could feel how the nanoskin had coalesced with my face. I could feel the wet, weepy rot on my left cheek. How had it been triggered? I didn't recall. Only, in this memory, I knew LYREBIRD was my only hope. Everyone else had died in those trials except me. And either Fyster would let me go, or LYREBIRD would free me. Either way, to escape him, I needed to threaten him.

"Let me go or I'll kill myself."

He looked at me. "And why should I care?"

"Because it works, you absolute bastard. My mind is

already in LYREBIRD. I've corrupted the tech." I don't think that was true. I think this was a bluff. But I banked on him not knowing I could be wiped; I wanted him to think of me as an infestation, already infecting every circuit in LYREBIRD. "You can either say I took the mask and ran, and let them hunt me down, or you can let me die and when VisorForge retrieves their product, my mind will tell them it was all your fault. And don't think about destroying it—they'll just fucking kill you if you do that." I was panting, breathing hard. "Well? Am I so stupid now?"

Fyster's throat bobbed as he swallowed. "I'm not letting you go, Sable."

I didn't wait a moment longer. I pulled the trigger.

Why did I kill myself like *that*? Fucking inefficient. Fucking slow. Surely, I'd known how drawn-out a stomach wound could be.

But I'd wanted Fyster to panic. I wanted him to dump me somewhere and flee to cover his tracks before Visor-Forge sent their goons to find me. More than that, I needed time to get that message out and call all those scavengers to me. I wanted to make sure someone found me, someone who'd be desperate to protect me. And I wanted to give LYREBIRD enough time to upload my mind into its stores, to really make sure I was still alive somewhere, that I wasn't killing myself for good.

I'd put every one of my hopes in the same basket and killed my body just for the chance of . . . living. Living as something else. Getting away from Fyster Alzian, making this life my own, even if that meant being a mind stored in a mask.

Out of the memory, Fyster was laughing at me. "Oh, you poor idiot copy. You think you're real, don't you?" He still thought I was lying. He still thought I wasn't Sable. That LYREBIRD's tech wasn't possible.

And if I was a copy, if I was code that believed itself to be real, then what was I?

What am I?

Where does my humanity end?

Fyster was saying, "You've managed to convince that sad sod outside that you were human once. But you never were. Dumb girl—you're just like her."

At least that was true. Whether I was truly Sable or not, I shared her rage. I shared the horror and the desperation, shared every heated desire that had led to this moment, and I still wanted, very badly, to kill Fyster Alzian.

So I did.

I reached out and clamped my hand around his throat. He jerked as if surprised—moments ago he had been out of my range, and I had closed the distance with inhuman speed, because neither of us was really here. I was a mask sitting on Fyster's head, I had no hands to squeeze his throat with. Even if the tactility was false, the feedback a lie, it felt good. It felt right. His eyes were bulging in his skull. He looked horrified. Righteous justice filled me.

But in truth, I was boiling his brain.

Outside of this construct, Fyster was howling. I blinked and was back in the room with you. Fyster writhed in the wingback chair. His mind pushed weakly against mine. With nowhere else to go, Fyster tried to infiltrate LYREBIRD, to take root in my home. Absolutely fucking not. I pushed back, I blocked every entrance, and Fyster hadn't endured VisorForge's trials. He had no idea how to work with this mask. He floundered and I felt him give up; a great pressure released and his mind retreated, faltering in his dying flesh. Pink, heated brain matter flooded from his ears in thick clumps. You were screaming too, Wylla—but you weren't angry with me. This was simply disgust.

Fyster spasmed once or twice, latent signals pulsing in his brain, but he was as good as dead. After it was done, I felt like singing.

"Ew," you whispered. "Ew. Sable. What the fuck."

I giggled. With euphoria pumping through my mind, every inhibition ebbed away, including any remnant of manners I still had. I enjoyed what I had done. The bastard deserved it.

Gingerly you reached over the chair and tried to tug me free only using a millimeter of your forefinger and thumb. LYREBIRD had now had the great pleasure of ending a marriage wholeheartedly.

"What happened?" you asked, taking me in your hands. I didn't reply. I didn't want to repeat outright everything Fyster had said, in case part of you thought he was right. I couldn't stand that. If I ended up being nothing more than a copy of a dead woman, what would you think of me then?

"Sable," you pressed. "Did you get the leverage?"

No.

You sighed. "Why not?"

You'll find out eventually. When you put me on.

You flipped over LYREBIRD and grumbled. Fyster's

eyes were smeared in LYREBIRD's sockets, so you weren't putting that on your face until you cleaned me out.

Your voice pitched high in annoyance. "Really?"

Just let me . . . feel this.

You stopped moving. You exhaled a little, because you hadn't let yourself feel it, either. Without hesitation, you had shot the security guard. You'd shot Fyster in the leg. And even when all that brain matter bubbled out of his ears and you were screaming, it wasn't quite out of fear.

I was elated, riding the afterglow. You had a barricade up, worried what it would mean if you enjoyed it too much. What kind of person that would make you.

For you, only part of this feeling had anything to do with the demise of Fyster Alzian. It was what he represented for you. A Corporate Federation darling brought to his knees before you; wouldn't it feel good to make the bastards suffer? Anyone who had ever thought badly of you. Anyone who had tried to control you. Anyone who had hoped for you to hurt.

Why the fuck should we stop here?

Let yourself feel it, I said. You unraveled a little, let your shoulders drop, let the feeling in, just enough to sprout. And you exhaled, this great sigh of relief.

It felt good, to accept a part of yourself that wasn't palatable. To stand up for yourself; to acknowledge that, deep inside you, beneath the Wylla that made herself small, who tried to be invisible, you were so incredibly angry.

Just like me.

But we couldn't linger long. You checked Fyster's

NAVIDAR, which still showed no VisorForge vessels in range. But at the door, we heard the first panicked knocking.

"Mr. Alzian? It's station security. Are you all right?"

Getting back to the docks that way would be nearly impossible. How much time did we have before security overrode your hack?

You said Fyster had a private dock and a ship. It needed biological material and an ID. His eyes are melted into me. Will that work?

You looked down at me and grimaced. My insides must have looked foul. "Replicate his ID. I'll take you to the door."

We couldn't leave without something more to show for it, but a way out took priority over information.

I'd gotten a good scan of Fyster and I replicated his ID now. The ship happily let me in, greeting me with an overly cheery, "Welcome, Fyster."

That made me feel rotten. Part of me worried some of him had wormed its way in, that somewhere in LYRE-BIRD's many circuits, a little pinch of Fyster Alzian had been preserved and would fester.

The ship was high-end. You whistled low at the sight of it, awed that it had a bridge, storage, and sleeping arrangements. The vessel was taller than it was long, presumably to accommodate someone of Fyster's height. Its engine room had several spare batteries, which made you elated; this vessel could be ours for a very long time.

Beautiful cream controls lit up from your touch. You spooled up the engine. Through LYREBIRD's eyes, you saw the insides of the ship and understood its mechanics. The knowledge came to you like a language you had learned long ago, a slow familiarity, until you were flicking switches and turning dials, and you grew fluent. The ship became yours.

But before you flew us out, you put me down on a panel in the bridge and typed away, using what time remained to dig into VisorForge.

You mirrored Fyster's work station and gave RABBIT the task of monitoring the NAVIDAR for VisorForge ships.

"We're on borrowed time. I can only mirror while we're docked and connected to his home system, so work fast."

Plug me into the computers. I'll search while you clean me.

So that's what we did.

Plugged in, I first scanned the station's systems. But even Fyster's clearance wasn't enough to see what alerts had come through from VisorForge, and I didn't want to waste your time on a hack when we knew they were coming for us. I moved on to his files.

I didn't know what I was looking for. Perhaps I had been too hasty in boiling Fyster's brain: he might have told me more about LYREBIRD if I'd kept him alive. But I was so fucking angry. And it was done, now.

Every file was encrypted, but Fyster's ID bypassed those locks. I almost wished it hadn't, to slow down the shock of self-discovery; within seconds I found a drive on the system marked *LYREBIRD* and I opened its contents all at once. Files of the deceased people in the trials.

Records of how their bodies broke, or how their minds went. How Sable Alzian survived initial testing; how her—my?—mind seeped into LYREBIRD's stores.

How it had copied.

Was that it, then? The truth? Was I a copy of Sable's mind? And now that she had killed her body, now that the original mind was dead, could I say that I was really her?

You came back with a wet cloth and grimly rubbed at the pink flesh coating LYREBIRD's insides. Some emotion must have leaked out of me because you flinched.

"What is it?"

Nothing, I thought quickly.

"Don't be silly, Sable," you whispered, admonishing. To hear you say my name, or her name—*that damn name*! It upset me. I seized up, went stiff; I have no idea how this translated, but you exhaled and lifted me up.

Then my search found correspondence, and everything changed. Before you could coo to me or calm me down, a new panic overcame me.

Put me on! I screamed at you. *Put me on right now!*

You did, hastily, pressing your face against the still-damp metal interior, cleaned as best as you could. We were both hit with overwhelming knowledge.

Firstly, everything Fyster had said to me flooded your mind. It fell into place as memory does, the information feeling simultaneously old and new as it slotted into your mind. You staggered back—confusion, apprehension, denial—this myriad of emotional forces swirled in your stomach. I worried you would listen to Fyster's doubt and think me inhuman, but you just said, "Show me what you found about VisorForge."

The trials had killed the bodies outright. We had both thought this was a mistake, that I was the sole proof that VisorForge's thesis could work. But I was the outlier—I was the mistake.

Dead bodies were always the intention.

Corporate Federation wanted to sell LYREBIRD technology, and the highest bidder would have been Martial Syndicate. What better way to maintain your ranks than letting the minds of dead soldiers pilot civilian bodies? What better way to make an empire than to use the people you encroach upon to kill their own worlds? Imagine a prisoner of war being forced to wear a LYREBIRD, and the mind stored in the mask mind leaking out. If they learned how to subdue the host mind as I had for you, then the dead could take over the living.

But had they worked out fusion? Did they understand how much more powerful it could be if two minds chose to become one?

We had slipped into each other while reading and now were breathing heavily. This changed everything: there were surely more LYREBIRDs than the one we wore. This future, this awful future, could still come to pass.

And the only situation we could think that this would benefit was war.

"With whom?"

"Independent planets and stations," I offered. "I don't know much about human settlements outside Corporate Federation sectors. But if our government is teaming up with Martial Syndicate, then it must be their intention."

A dull banging sounded and we turned to see three

security guards pressed against the sealed docking door. Before we could react, RABBIT trilled loudly just as a single VisorForge vessel popped onto the NAVIDAR.

You went to disengage Fyster's ship from the dock immediately, but something made you pause.

"No," you hissed, and when I realized, time seemed to slow.

The station's comms warbled as they were taken over, and the voice that came through was flat and hollow. With mechanical precision it said, *"This is VisorForge Subsidiary Four. Wylla Sotain, surrender immediately. You will be pursued until the contraband is retrieved."*

A further four vessels jumped into range, but it was the first one that terrified you.

Fyster hadn't been lying.

A Subsidiary had come for us.

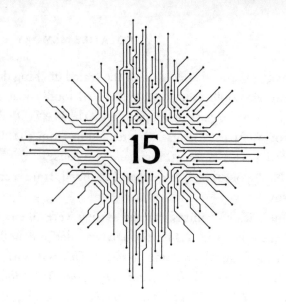

15

You took a deep breath and centered yourself before the controls.

"You're a brilliant mimic, Sable," you said, voice ringing. "An incredible thing. Let's show Visor-Forge how incomparable you are."

"*We* are." Hearing your praise made me sing those words. I knew immediately what you wanted us to do.

The Subsidiary spoke again: "*Wylla Sotain, we will be docking in T-minus three minutes. Present yourself in GSC-05's dock.*"

You pulled up the viewer. VisorForge had spread all their ships out in a perfect flank. The engine on Fyster's ship was practically silent as it whirred to life. You steered us off the dock. Immediately, we were hailed. You ignored it, but our systems crackled and the Subsidiary's voice came through once more. "*If you are an innocent party, I suggest you return to dock. VisorForge has requested complete cooperation from GSC-05 citizens. Failure to comply will authorize us to shoot you down.*"

You opened a channel and we pulled him from the viscous gore, from the outskirts of LYREBIRD's mind; we embodied Fyster Alzian not as the cowering, broken man he had become, but as I remembered him.

"Hail, Subsidiary Four," we said gruffly. "This is Fyster Alzian, VisorForge Employee ID number C-2031–99-M-42-VML. There's no need to dock. I have subdued the fugitive; VisorForge tech has been retrieved unharmed."

Barely a moment passed before we got a response. RABBIT reported the VisorForge vessels were moving— but not to intercept. They began to trail us as we passed, herding us closer to the waiting Subsidiary vessel.

"Very good, Mr. Alzian. We thank you for your co-operation; you are a valued member of the VisorForge family. Please align your vessel and we will commence boarding to retrieve the fugitive."

We clicked off the comms. You exhaled noisily; our shared heart raced.

You asked, "What do you know about Subsidiaries?"

I knew legends, myths, nothing substantial, but I listed off abilities anyway. "I've heard everything from quantum teleportation to adaptive camouflage without use of a CHAMELEON. Some stories say cybernetic enhancements for enhanced speed and strength. Neural hacking if they touch you. Emotion suppression so they thrive in high-stress environments. Regenerative nano-bots, so they're hard to kill. Something about tracking."

"They can track if they have proximity to jumping ships. I've heard that one, too." For a tight moment, you said nothing. "We have to get out of range before we jump."

You upped the thrusters minutely and pulled up the

system, repurposing the code you'd used to shield Ork-it's gun from the station lock. You were trying to hide the jump drive from the Subsidiary's sensors. We needed to spool it up without being noticed. With shaking hands, you pressed the button, and it began to whir to life.

We waited tensely for a minute. The vessels were still shepherding us. I thought we had done it until RABBIT trilled. Heat signatures appeared on the NAVIDAR and seconds later two warning shots skimmed the hull. The vessel shook.

"*Shit*," you spat. The vessel reported no damage. They were well aimed—not at all intended to harm us.

You took control of the ship and slammed forward at full thruster speed, veering us away from the Subsidiary vessel. The VisorForge ships matched us immediately. Our heart raced; you focused on an exact point in the black of space, the very distance you estimated would be out of the Subsidiary's tracking range.

You glanced down at the NAVIDAR. Our dot of a ship beeped steadily away from the others. We hadn't cleared the range yet; the system showed us red. Red. And then—

The ship shuddered and everything went white. All electronics died with an EMP.

It was nothing like the weak scavenger's pulse that had stunned the Military Syndicate vessel. This blast ripped me away from you. For one dizzying moment, I spun in nothingness. I had to fight my way back to you through stunned neural synapses.

When I returned to LYREBIRD, you'd managed to work through the disorientation. You had rushed to the engine room and rerouted a series of cables. We became one just as you pulled a spare engine battery into the middle of the room.

I now knew why you'd been so pleased at the sight of the spare batteries; Orkit's EMP had left us dead in the water, but with a spare battery, we now had a chance.

Cables in hand, you rushed back to the console and pulled up some code, mumbling, "Okay, okay," over and over.

"What do you need?" I asked.

"Time."

"I'll need to use your voice," I whispered. "Do I have your permission?"

"Yes," you said.

"Open the channel," I said.

"Let's do this. You and I."

And we split.

It was like how I had split between LYREBIRD and the android body on BTW-02, only this time, your bodily functions were governed by separate brains. Your mind used your fingers to code, and I distracted the Subsidiary through the comms.

In its own voice—that flat, eerie monotone—I said, "Subsidiary Four, this is Subsidiary Four. You don't want to shoot this vessel down, or you would have already. You need LYREBIRD intact. So, Four, I am calling your bluff."

In the seconds it took the Subsidiary to reply, I tried something. I sent part of my mind through the hail until I was on the fringes of the Subsidiary vessel's system. With Fyster's vessel ID in hand, I gently suggested to the Subsidiary ship that there were three of us. Or four. Or ten—I threw mixed signals into its NAVIDAR in the hope it would momentarily confuse it.

I don't know if it worked. The Subsidiary was saying, "*Wylla Sotain, cease emulation immediately. The tech you use is dangerous.*"

And you, Wylla, you had finished your programming. We came together in a beautiful rush and in your own voice you proclaimed, "I am not using her. We are one. And you have no idea how dangerous we can be."

The spare battery had finished powering up the jump drive. Perhaps we were still close enough to track, but we could buy ourselves time. We'd jump again and again until we lost it.

The Subsidiary must have known. The closest thing to anger that it could muster laced its monotone cry. "*Wait—!*"

We jumped.

You didn't stop there, jumping five times for good measure even as the battery whirred from overuse. You put us a whole sector away and only then did you let yourself breathe a sigh of relief.

My brilliant Wylla, you had saved us.

We sat in silence for minutes, processing first the existence of Subsidiaries and the inevitable bounty on our shared head, and then the information I'd gleaned from Fyster's files.

The Corporate Federation and the Martial Syndicate were planning something.

We were connected. You reached for me and I reached back; an intangible embrace. "So what do we do?"

What a question. What a sprawling, heavy question. Were we to decide the rest of our lives in that moment?

You prompted me again, even though you could hear those swirling thoughts. "What do you want to do, Sable?"

I balked. "You're still going to call me that?"

"You're Sable to me." My heart leaped, Wylla, when you spoke so certainly. "Is that all right?"

Breathlessly I answered, "Yes."

You looked down at your hands. "I know it wouldn't be the same. I know, but I could . . . I could make good on that promise. Find an android body for you."

And then I would be a copy of a copy in an android body, another degree removed from the humanity I remembered, and I didn't want that.

"I want to be with you," I whispered. "That's all I know."

"I think," you whispered back, "I want that, too."

I thought about you kissing me.

And you thought about kissing me.

Somewhere, somehow, in the liminal space between our minds and our physical forms, I thought it might be possible. I could make a construct the way Fyster's mind made his. I could walk to you.

I could kiss you.

I knew we didn't have much time. VisorForge was hunting us. But you had weaved us through VisorForge ships and you'd spoken back to a Subsidiary, and that lit a kind of delicious fire in me. I wanted to take your hand and jump and revel and shout. You had saved us from VisorForge. You had saved me from Fyster. I was free of him. I could love who I wanted to. I was free of him, and I could kiss you, and I still felt angry. Why did I still feel angry?

"It's okay," you said.

I blinked, and I saw you, standing ahead of me. And I flinched, because I looked down and had hands, feet, a body. Immediately, I wanted to throw up. Everything was easier when you couldn't see me; I think, in that moment, I understood why you tried so often to hide. Being seen, truly, was too much. I was a violent little creature, and now I was a woman. Was that the same thing? All that anger, all that impossible emotion.

I was shaking. You stepped forward and took my hand and squeezed it. I squeezed back. You stepped closer. My mind generated the warmth of your body; I felt your hand wrap around my waist. Inexplicably, I had the urge to bite my own arm. To consume myself, gnaw away at this feeling, break open the vessel containing it.

"Calm down," you said, like you were any better than me at self-regulating. I covered my face; you reached out and peeled away my fingers, and you were so close all I had to do was close my eyes and step forward.

So I did.

It was gentle and it was wanting. I tried to inhale you. In truth, you were wearing me, we were fused; there was no way to get any closer. But I wanted to be inside you, cradled in the safety of your rib cage, close to that heart of yours. I wanted to eat it, I wanted to be it. I wanted to get so close to you we wouldn't be able to see the seams.

Was that desire unhealthy?

I shivered and the construct fell away.

We had decided. This. Us. We both wanted that. Whatever happened.

After a moment in that quiet, you opened up the GIRS. Your body moved without order, so I didn't catch what was happening until you were erasing the record. Your record. You wiped yourself from the GIRS completely.

Wylla Sotain, ID number N-7210–86–F-28–S.

Not just dead. Gone.

I didn't understand. Wylla, you had purged yourself. Everything you had ever done and everything you had ever been—years of your life spent cultivating this identity. Every skill you had learned to maintain it, every credit spent, every hour—and you had chosen to start again. All your effort to doctor it, urging whoever looked to see Wylla, and not what you used to be. Now, you would rely on your own body for the first time: you would let people look at you and determine your gender. Wylla existed only in memories now. How would you do anything? How would you dock anywhere, how would you upgrade your vessel? Your credits existed only on RAB-BIT, now. If anyone got ahold of it, you would have no money to your name.

A perfect, highly skilled unstitching; you made it look like you had never existed at all.

Wylla was dead.

"What?" I murmured. "What have you done?"

"It's fine," you said. Your heart rate said otherwise; it pounded against your chest in a panic, but you kept yourself impassive and calm. "I chose this. I chose you. Us. And that—version of me . . . What could I do anyway, if I kept it? My identifier is everywhere. As soon as we landed, or did anything, they would know."

Incredulous, I asked, "And now? Now you have nothing?"

"Sable Veonya, did you forget all the incredible things you can do?"

My panic had made me slow. Here I was worried that you would be this nameless vagabond floating around in space until you died, never able to dock, or refuel, or restock—you had made yourself a slow suicide. But then I thought: *Oh.* Because Wylla, you were smarter than me, and perhaps you could feel it as innately as I could feel your heartbeat. Somewhere in this fusion, we had both unlocked each other.

We would be invisible; we would be whoever LYREBIRD spoofed.

And now you could be Wylla without the weight of your birth.

"So?" you said. "Where are we going?"

"To give them hell," I said. The bastards behind LYREBIRD deserved to have their brains boiled, too.

We moved together, one body secure in the haven of this ship. You set a course to anywhere.

Adrenaline gave way to something else; a spark of joy. Perhaps I was corrupting you, but I thought you were having fun.

"You know we'll be running a very long time?" I asked.

And you, brilliant Wylla, laughed. "Then let's stop running. Why don't we fight?"

ACKNOWLEDGMENTS

If Pamela Freeman hadn't told me to take a break and write something entirely out of my comfort zone, *Volatile Memory* wouldn't exist. She said I needed distance from an ambitious project I began at eighteen and still haven't finished, and she was right. A huge thank-you to Pamela and the Australian Writers' Centre, and I suppose to myself for investing in that course all those years ago.

Wylla was the first creation in *Volatile Memory*'s world, and she breathed from the first speed-written exercise I cranked out in 2019. Thank you to all the writers who have pushed the genre in the years before me and allowed me to get weird in this novella.

Many thanks to my agent, Maeve MacLysaght, for reading the first iteration on a plane and emailing me upon landing with excitement. You always champion me and my work, and I couldn't do this without you.

To Oliver Dougherty, you are precisely the editor for this project. I am so grateful that I get to work with someone whose vision aligns with my own. Thank you for pushing *Volatile Memory* to be its best.

To the entire Tordotcom team, thank you for embracing

Sable and Wylla's story. Your enthusiasm and hard work mean a lot.

To my father, for always being so honest with my writing that I glowed when you told me this was the best thing I've ever written.

To my mother, for taking care of me as I wrote this.

To my darling Shaz: This was the last book of mine you left your pawprints on. Thank you for nearly nineteen years.

To my friends, namely Chrissie, Ellie, and Gemma, for your ongoing support.

And finally to my partner, Beau. I am blessed to have you in my corner. Thank you for believing in me, supporting my dreams, and shoring me up whenever I have doubts. You are my family.

ABOUT THE AUTHOR

SETH HADDON is the queer Australian writer of *Reforged, Reborn,* and *Reclaimed.* He is a video game designer and producer, has a degree in ancient history, and previously worked with cats. Some of his previous adventures include exploring Pompeii with a famous archaeologist and being chased through a train station by a nun.

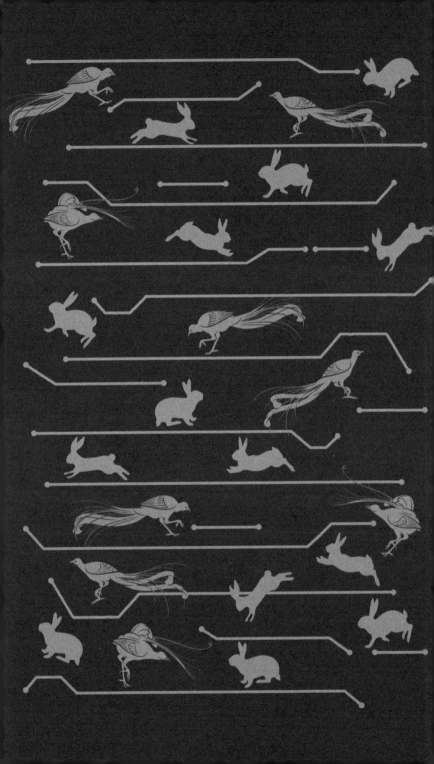